✳ "You haven't told .... n looking for m

The .... don't know?"

Tim ..

"I tho..... ..... you were magic you knew all kinds of stuff."

"Don't I wish." Ever since Tim had discovered that he was magic, he'd continually felt like a sham. Everyone acted like he had all this power, and maybe he did—or would—but he sure didn't know how to use it. Or how to do anything much. He shook his head. "That's not how it is. All it really is is confusing. And complicated. And people all seem to want something—like to kill me."

Then it sunk in—she knew he was magic. He went back on alert. "You don't want to kill me, do you?" He peered at the apple through his glasses.

The girl giggled. "Of course not."

"Then why are you here? And how do you know I'm, well, magic?"

"There's a place," she said, "a place where we can go when we need someplace to go. That's why I'm here."

"We?"

"People who aren't grown-ups yet. Kids. Us. Kerwyn says it's a sanctuary, but it's really just a place. We call it Free Country." ✳

the BOOKS of MAGIC ∗ 3
™

The Children's Crusade

Carla Jablonski

Created by
Neil Gaiman and John Bolton

BOOKS FOR
VERTIGO
YOUNG ADULTS

eos

An Imprint of HarperCollinsPublishers

Eos is an imprint of HarperCollins Publishers.

This is a work of fiction. Any resemblance to any real people (living, dead, or
stolen by fairies), or to any real animals, gods, witches, countries, and events
(magical or otherwise), is just blind luck, or so we hope.

Library of Congress Cataloging-in-Publication Data
Jablonski, Carla.
   The children's crusade / Carla Jablonski ; created by Neil Gaiman and John
Bolton.— 1st Eos ed.
      p.   cm. — (The books of magic ; #3)
   Adapted from the serialized story in the Books of Magic originally published by
Vertigo, 1994.
   Sequel: Consequences.
   Summary: Thirteen-year-old Tim Hunter is lured through a magic gate to Free
Country, a place of refuge for children, where he uses his magic to thwart a hidden
evil.
   ISBN 0-06-447381-3 (pbk.)
   [1. Magic—Fiction. 2. Wizards—Fiction. 3. England—Fiction.] I. Gaiman, Neil.
II. Bolton, John, 1951– III. Books of magic. IV. Title.
PZ7.J1285 Ch 2003   2003007547
[Fic]—dc21   CIP
                                                                AC

Typography by R. Hult
❖

First Eos edition, 2003
Visit us on the World Wide Web!
www.harpereos.com
www.dccomics.com

For my mom and dad, who created
Free Country on the Upper West Side.
—CJ

THE BOOKS OF MAGIC
An Introduction

by Neil Gaiman

WHEN I WAS STILL a teenager, only a few years older than Tim Hunter is in the book you are holding, I decided it was time to write my first novel. It was to be called *Wild Magic*, and it was to be set in a minor British Public School (which is to say, a private school), like the ones from which I had so recently escaped, only a minor British Public School that taught magic. It had a young hero named Richard Grenville, and a pair of wonderful villains who called themselves Mister Croup and Mister Vandemar. It was going to be a mixture of Ursula K. Le Guin's *A Wizard of Earthsea* and T. H. White's *The Sword in the Stone*, and, well, me, I suppose. That was the plan. It seemed to me that learning about magic was the perfect story, and I was sure I could really write convincingly about school.

I wrote about five pages of the book before I realized that I had absolutely no idea what I was doing, and I stopped. (Later, I learned that most books are actually written by people who have no idea what they are doing, but go on to finish writing the books anyway. I wish I'd known that then.)

Years passed. I got married, and had children of my own, and learned how to finish writing the things I'd started.

Then one day in 1988, the telephone rang.

It was an editor in America named Karen Berger. I had recently started writing a monthly comic called *The Sandman*, which Karen was editing, although no issues had yet been published. Karen had noticed that I combined a sort of trainspotterish knowledge of minor and arcane DC Comics characters with a bizarre facility for organizing them into something more or less coherent. And also, she had an idea.

"Would you write a comic," she asked, "that would be a history of magic in the DC Comics universe, covering the past and the present and the future? Sort of a Who's Who, but with a story? We could call it *The Books of Magic*."

I said, "No, thank you." I pointed out to her how silly an idea it was—a Who's Who and a history and a travel guide that was also a story. "Quite a ridiculous idea," I said, and she apologized for having suggested it.

In bed that night I hovered at the edge of sleep, musing about Karen's call, and what a ridiculous idea it was. I mean . . . a story that would go from the beginning of time . . . to the end of time . . . and have someone meet all these strange people . . . and learn all about magic. . . .

Perhaps it wasn't so ridiculous. . . .

And then I sighed, certain that if I let myself sleep it would all be gone in the morning. I climbed out of bed and crept through the house back to my office, trying not to wake anyone in my hurry to start scribbling down ideas.

A boy. Yes. There had to be a boy. Someone smart and funny, something of an outsider, who would learn that he had the potential to be the greatest magician the world had ever seen—more powerful than Merlin. And four guides, to take him through the past, the present, through other worlds, through the future, serving the same function as the ghosts who accompany Ebenezer Scrooge through Charles Dickens's *A Christmas Carol.*

I thought for a moment about calling him Richard Grenville, after the hero of my book-I'd-never-written, but that seemed a rather too heroic name (the original Sir Richard Grenville was a seacaptain, adventurer, and explorer, after all). So I called him Tim, possibly because the Monty

Python team had shown that Tim was an unlikely sort of name for an enchanter, or with faint memories of the hero of Margaret Storey's magical children's novel, *Timothy and Two Witches*. I thought perhaps his last name should be Seekings, and it was, in the first outline I sent to Karen—a faint tribute to John Masefield's haunting tale of magic and smugglers, *The Midnight Folk*. But Karen felt this was a bit literal, so he became, in one stroke of the pen, Tim Hunter.

And as Tim Hunter he sat up, blinked, wiped his glasses on his T-shirt, and set off into the world.

(I never actually got to use the minor British Public School that taught only magic in a story, and I suppose now I never will. But I was very pleased when Mr. Croup and Mr. Vandemar finally showed up in a story about life under London, called *Neverwhere*.)

John Bolton, the first artist to draw Tim, had a son named James who was just the right age and he became John's model for Tim, tousle-haired and bespectacled. And in 1990 the first four volumes of comics that became the first *Books of Magic* graphic novel were published.

Soon enough, it seemed, Tim had a monthly series of comics chronicling his adventures and misadventures, and the slow learning process he was to undergo, as initially chronicled by author John Ney Reiber, who gave Tim a number of things—most importantly, Molly.

In this new series of novels-without-pictures, Carla Jablonski has set herself a challenging task: not only adapting Tim's stories, but also telling new ones, and through it all illuminating the saga of a young man who might just grow up to be the most powerful magician in the world. If, of course, he manages to live that long. . . .

Neil Gaiman
May 2002

Prologue

*T*HE YEAR WAS 1212. *The fourth crusade had come to a bloody end. The result had been every bit as successful as the previous three, which is to say it had been a complete and utter failure. For over a hundred years, armies had marched on the holy city, but Jerusalem was still in the hands of the Saracens.*

Then a man in the garb of a holy monk rose up among the people of France and Germany. He preached a dark gospel to them all.

"Why have all the crusades failed?" he demanded. "Even with the might and love and power of God on our side, why do our armies always fall to the heathens? Why?"

His dark eyes flashed at the stunned and silent crowd. "Because we are not pure!" he answered for them. His voice thundered with the timbre of the righteous. "Because our soldiers are already soiled and stained with sin. How can we sinners win for ourselves the Holy Land?" He paused, letting the sinners before him contemplate the question. "How? I tell you how! We must raise an army of innocents. An army of children. And when they reach Jerusalem, with God and innocence on their side, our victory shall be assured. This will be the greatest of all of the holy wars. This will be the Children's Crusade!"

The crowd murmured and mumbled and slowly dispersed. He had held them enthralled until he pronounced his solution; after that they dismissed him. But they spoke of him and his mad plan.

The words of the monk were transmitted across Europe. Adults scoffed, but the children heard—and believed. Throughout the continent children huddled together, whispering, planning, thinking, yearning. They flocked to the crusade. Some left their parents and their comfortable homes. Others left alleys, farms, and forests.

Over fifty thousand boys and girls traveled to Marseilles, where one hundred ships waited for them. None of the children knew where Jerusalem was, nor what would happen when they got there, but their faith sustained them. The man dressed as the monk stood at the docks and watched the children board the ships. And he smiled.

The ships set sail in January 1213. Over the next few months, children continued to arrive in Marseilles, hoping to join the crusade. But once those one hundred ships had set sail, none were to follow.

The late arrivals wept at the shore, heartbroken that they could not be part of the army of God.

They were the lucky ones.

A great storm came up and destroyed ninety-eight of the hundred ships. Forty-nine thousand children drowned that night. It could be argued that they, too, were the lucky ones. For the hundred ships were not bound for Jerusalem but for the port of Anfa in Morocco. And the children were not to be the champions of a holy war but chattel in a thriving slave trade.

The remaining two ships arrived in Morocco and were met by a smiling man who was no longer dressed as a monk. Eight hundred children (two hundred had died during passage) were unloaded and sold in the port marketplace. Word of the children's fate slowly trickled back to Europe. The identity of the monk who began the affair was never discovered.

Fifty thousand children departed for the crusade. None of them ever returned home.

Aiken Drum and his sister, Mwyfany, marched across the burning sands. They had survived the storms, but they were now in a strange land. They had traveled so far for so long; Aiken could no longer remember how long. First there had been the excitement of joining the Crusade. They were to do great things! They were going to become important, a part of something so much larger than themselves. This excitement and purpose propelled them to Marseilles, and their faith was what sustained them once on board the ship.

Aiken and his sister knew no fear at first. And even as the great ship lurched and rolled, even as they shivered together, imagining the horrors that the war they were about to join might bring, they remained brave, for they knew they were on the side of all that was good and right and true. Their God would protect them. After all, it was for Him and His glory that they had undertaken this great journey. If their treatment by the crew was rough, or indifferent at best, the eager children thought nothing of it. Taking care of the ship was far more important than taking care of them, they reasoned.

That was before the others drowned. And before their own arrival in Morocco.

The sun parched Aiken's throat. His lips were cracked, and his skin was tight and burned. He glanced down the line, where his sister stumbled, dragged along by the larger children in front of her. His sister was worse off than he. She was such a little thing, and they'd had nothing to eat for such a long time. He saw a shadow in the sand and forced himself to face forward again, avoiding another crack of the whip.

They had been sold, like the rest of the remaining survivors of the voyage, in the clamor of the marketplace. Mwyfany had cowered against him, frightened by the words shouted at them in strange languages, the pungent aromas, and peculiar wares. At first, Aiken counted himself lucky that he and Mwyfany had not been separated. But now he wondered if she would have been better off sold to a different master. Aiken had no idea where they were going, and he wasn't sure if they would survive getting there. Maybe someone else would have put her to work in a kitchen or a laundry. Too late now.

How long would this forced march go on? he wondered again and again as the sand scraped the bottom of his feet and the sun made his eyes burn.

The journey seemed endless. The nights were bitter cold, and the limited amount of drinking water was foul. And, yet, none of the thirteen children trudging across the desert turned their burned and peeling faces from their faith. They still believed in miracles.

"Aiken!" Mwyfany called.

Aiken twisted to see his sister, the ropes chafing at his wrists. She had fallen and was struggling to stand up. Her efforts were dragging down the children around her. The captors released her from the ropes that tied her to the others. She still could not stand. The captors cracked a whip to keep the line moving. They left her where she was, digging at the sand, trying to get up.

"No!" Aiken cried. He dug in his heels and stopped. One of the men whipped him, and for good measure whipped the boy in front of him and the girl behind, making sure they kept picking up their feet.

"Mwyfany!" Aiken cried. "Mwyfany!"

The stinging whip, the searing sand, and his own weakened body betrayed him. All conspired to keep him from stopping for her, from fighting. He could not even say a prayer—or good-bye.

Her voice was so faint, like the patter of autumn leaves drifting across the ground. Aiken felt like he would murder their captors, were it not for the ropes that tied him to his fellow child slaves.

The tears he cried for his sister trickled down his dirty cheeks, but he made no sound. His body shuddered as he struggled to keep the racking sobs from exploding out of him.

He felt a soft touch on his back, and his head whipped around. Gazing into the dark eyes of the girl behind him, Aiken saw sympathy and sorrow. She touched him again, letting him know she understood his pain and then jerked her head, indicating he should look forward again or face the whip.

On and on. On and on. They traveled across the desert and then by water, then across a forest. Late one starless night, they came to a city and were led through dark streets into a huge building. Once inside, they were pushed down into a cellar and were left there in the dark.

There were twelve of them now: twelve exhausted, filthy, frightened, starving children. None was over the age of fourteen.

Slowly, they edged their way into understanding one another—a few words of French, English, Italian, or Spanish here and there. Some of the boys spoke a little Latin. Eventually, with this strange amalgam of languages they created a new one of their own design. They whispered together, offering comfort, and wondered about their fate.

Aiken learned that the dark-eyed girl was named Yolande and that she had come from Spain with her sister. She didn't tell him why she was alone now; she didn't have to. Her braids were matted, and her face was thin and haggard from the journey. He guessed her to be about ten years old—just midway between his age and Mwyfany's—but their ordeal had given her the look of a wizened old creature. He supposed he must look far older than his own fourteen years.

It was impossible to tell what was day and what was night in the pit. From time to time the trapdoor opened and someone threw down rotten meat or spoiled fruit. Water was lowered in a bucket once a day. And as time passed, the smell in the pit grew worse and worse. They lived in the dark, and never knew how much time was passing.

Then one day some men came down and took Yolande away.

Aiken sat in the pit, his back against the slimy wall, and listened with the others. Yolande's screams sent chills along his spine. And then came sudden silence, which was even worse. The children looked at one another in the little bit of light that made its way into the cellar, acknowledging with growing horror that they now knew their futures.

Somehow, maybe in response to his terror, Aiken fell asleep. He hadn't even begun to dream when he awoke with a start. Yolande stood before him, speaking in his own language, though she had never learned more than a few words of it. "There is a way out," she told him. "There is a place to go, where you will always be safe." And then she showed him how.

He blinked, and she was gone. He peered into the darkness and saw shining wide-awake eyes all around him. Yolande had appeared to them all and had spoken to each in his native tongue.

"A gate," she had promised them. And now they knew how to open it.

"We'll do it now," Aiken said in the language they had created. Nods went around the circle.

"We should have a leader," someone said.

How to choose? This was not a time for making speeches or taking votes. The simplest methods are always the best. Around the circle they went, playing rock, paper, scissor, eliminating a player with each turn. Paper covers rock; scissor cuts paper, rock crushes scissor. Finally it came down to Aiken and the boy named Kerwyn. He was the oldest, a little older than Aiken.

Aiken looked into the tall boy's eyes and knew his own mind. He did not want to win the round. He was too afraid and too weary to be a leader. First his sister, then Yolande. He had lost too much to be responsible for the safety of others. On a hunch, behind his back, he formed his fingers into the scissor shape.

"One, two, three, shoot," someone called out, and the two boys held out their hands. Aiken displayed his scissor.

Kerwyn's hand was balled into a fist: He had chosen rock. Kerwyn was the leader.

They settled into a circle, and Kerwyn took

his knife and cut each child's finger. They used this blood to draw the special pattern Yolande had described on the floor. Sometimes Kerwyn had to cut the children more than once in order to have enough blood. Creating this door to freedom had its cost. They were the first; they had to give of themselves to break through. And the ritual bound them together as blood brothers and sisters.

Finally, they were ready. Kerwyn was the first to dance the pattern. The hopscotch grid glowed crimson red—and he vanished! It had worked!

Aiken thought of his sister. If only . . . He shook his head. It was too late now for wishing. One by one, the children hopped the pattern and disappeared. Aiken approached the hopscotch grid. He took a deep breath and jumped . . .

. . . into Free Country. Where nothing could ever hurt them again.

Chapter One

I wish I could tell Molly all of what's going on. But how can I? I can't exactly say "Sorry, Moll, but I've been kind of busy being attacked by weird and not always human strangers and finding out my dad's not my dad but actually this bird guy, and, oh yes, there was that little bit there where I nearly died but saved all of Faerie.

Still, she's the one I usually tell everything to—everything I can, that is. The other stuff, well, that's between me and you. Oh man! Now I'm talking to a bloody journal!

Anyway.

She was really great when I went to her with that big news—the dad-not-being-my-dad part. Only what I haven't told her about is the magic. And that's the biggest whammy of them all. So while she knows that my mother was pregnant when she married Dad—I mean, Mr. Hunter—she doesn't know that my real father was a guy who could turn into a bird. Or that I've been back and forth between worlds, visiting the land of Faerie, where my real father lives.

Tim looked down at his journal and bit the end of his pencil. He scratched out the last word he'd written and replaced it with "lived."

He sat back hard against his desk chair and shut his eyes behind his glasses. "It's not fair," he murmured. "In fact, it bloody well rots."

Tim hadn't simply *visited* Faerie that last time—he had actually saved the entire alternate world from the grip of the evil creature known as the manticore. It was in performing that little act of heroism that he'd gotten himself killed, although thanks to some magic bargaining, it was Tamlin who wound up permanently dead.

Tamlin, the Queen's Falconer, who also happened to be Tim's real father, had sacrificed his life so Tim could live, performing a spell that allowed him to trade places with Tim, who was near death. It meant Tim would never get any answers to the enormous questions that pounded in his brain. It made everything so confusing.

But Tim was also intensely grateful. He knew he would be dead right now if it hadn't been for what Tamlin had done.

How am I ever going to sort things out? Tim wondered. *Like, how did he ever meet my mum?*

It was awfully difficult for Tim to picture his mother and Tamlin together. Tim didn't imagine that they'd met at some sort of singles gathering, like groups had at the community center. Not likely that there would have been a special "humans and birds" night. That brought up another question: Did his mum even know that she had gotten herself pregnant by a guy who spent part of his time as a hawk and lived full-time in Faerie?

There were no answers. Only more questions. And the fact that Tim had recently discovered that he had the potential to become the most powerful magician of his time didn't help. After that, all bloody hell had broken loose: He'd been attacked,

admired, confused, and amazed in an extremely
compressed amount of time.

*If Tamlin were still here, he could help me under-
stand my magic*, Tim thought wistfully. *That's kind
of what a dad does, isn't it? Helps you figure out who
you are and how to be in the world.*

Tim snorted. *Not that I would know what a dad
does.* He cocked his head, listening. Yup, the telly
was still blaring downstairs. That was how the
bloke he previously believed was his father—Mr.
Hunter—spent most of his time, since the car
accident that had killed Tim's mum and taken one
of his father's arms.

"Magic." Tim stood up and paced his small
room. If only he understood his powers better. Or
understood what it really meant to have all this
potential. *And while I'm making wishes*, Tim
thought, *it would be really great if the whole world
wasn't out to get me.* It wasn't just the magical
world that was fraught with danger and ene-
mies—his teachers seemed to be on his case constantly these days, too.

He shut his journal and pulled his algebra
test from his backpack. "Maybe I have been a
little distracted," he muttered, glaring at the
bright red C– at the top of the page. "But who
could blame me?" He didn't think a single other
bloke in school was dealing with quite as much as

he was. Maybe he *should* spill it all to Molly. He could use an ally.

Okay. Maybe he'd risk it—surely she'd understand. He grabbed a jacket and bounded down the stairs. Knowing he was going to finally have someone to talk to about this whole magic thing gave him energy to spare. So what if he didn't have any idea what words to use to convince Molly he wasn't completely mad. Whatever he said, he knew Molly would listen. And if she decided he was a loon after all, well, then, she wasn't the kind of friend he thought she was in the first place.

"I'm going out, Dad," Tim called as he passed the dark living room.

His dad gazed at the flickering light on the TV screen. "You're missing a good one, Tim," his dad said without looking up. "Come watch this girl dance."

Mr. Hunter liked those big movie musicals from the old days—the ones filled with pretty girls kicking their legs in unison or tap-dancing on pianos or some such.

"No thanks, Dad," Tim said.

Mr. Hunter finally glanced up and gave Tim a small smile. Not too long ago, he had confirmed Tim's suspicions, admitting that Tim's mother had already been pregnant by another man when she and Mr. Hunter had married. Since then, Mr. Hunter had been a lot more tentative around Tim. Gentle, almost. He was certainly paying more attention. Tim hadn't decided yet if that was a good thing or a bad thing.

"Good for you, then," Mr. Hunter said. "Good to see you out and about."

"That's me, social butterfly," Tim said. "See you."

He left the house and headed for Molly's, sprinting all the way. He rang the doorbell and bounced a little on his toes. He felt nervous about what he was about to do. It wasn't as if the Trenchcoat Brigade—the four blokes who had introduced him to magic in the first place—had told him it was a super secret or anything. But he knew it wasn't the kind of thing a chap ought to spread around.

Molly can keep a secret, he reminded himself. *All I have to do is convince her that it's true. That this whole magic thing isn't a psycho reaction to finding out I'm not my dad's son.*

Molly opened the door with her coat on. "Hey, Tim. Want to go to the library?"

"The library?" Tim repeated. "On a Saturday?"

A tall, chubby girl stood behind Molly. She was also wearing a coat. "I'm Becca, Molly's cousin. I'm driving her to the big library down-town."

"Oh." Tim shifted from foot to foot on the doorstep. This wasn't what he'd planned at all.

"I'm going to go find those keys, then we'll head out," Becca told Molly. She disappeared back into the kitchen.

"So do you want to come?" Molly asked.

"Nah," Tim said. "Why are you going to the downtown library? There's one right close by."

"The little one here is so ratty," Molly com-plained. "All the books have stains and the pages are falling out. And the books I wanted were already checked out at school."

"What are you working on?" Tim asked, won-dering if there was some school assignment he had totally spaced on.

"My paper for history," she replied. "We're studying the Industrial Revolution. I'm going to write about child labor laws."

Tim nodded, grateful that he was in a differ-ent history section from Molly and hadn't been assigned a paper yet.

"Hey, what's your theory about the missing kids?" Molly asked.

"The what?" Tim asked. "What missing kids?"

Molly's brown eyes grew wide. "How could

you have missed it? Everyone at school was talking about it." Then her expression grew concerned.
"I suppose you've had a lot on your mind." Molly
knew that Tim was still reeling from having discovered who his father was.

"Kind of," Tim admitted.

"Still, I'm surprised you haven't heard it on
the telly or the radio."

"Dad doesn't like the news. He prefers his old
movies. All black-and-white for him." Tim sighed.
That summed up his dad, all right. Mr. Hunter
lived in a black-and-white world. Tim had the feeling that Tamlin, his real father, had been fully
technicolor.

"Well, some kids vanished from a town not
too far from here," Molly explained, "all at once.
No one knows what to make of it."

"Sounds weird."

Molly nodded. "It's like one of those unsolved
mysteries on TV."

The door opened. "Come on, let's go," Becca
said. "You coming?" she asked Tim.

Tim shook his head. He didn't feel like tagging along with Molly just to go to a library where
they'd have to be quiet. And Molly would want to
study. For some reason she liked school.

What a letdown. Tim felt like a balloon losing
its air. He had geared himself up to share this

huge secret with Molly, got himself brave enough to do it, had charged over here, and now . . . nothing. He'd have to either give up on telling her or go through the whole process of revving himself up all over again.

Molly must have noticed his expression. "Don't look so glum," she scolded with a teasing smile. "Things could be worse. You could be living back when you'd have to work in some factory like these kids I'm writing about. They'd work eleven-, twelve-hour days and be grateful for a crust of bread and a few pennies."

"Come on, if we're going," Becca barked at Molly. "I've got work to do myself."

"See you later, Tim," Molly said.

"Okay."

Tim watched them climb into Becca's beat-up old car, uncertain of what to do. Should he go back home again? He didn't feel like being cooped up. Preparing himself to tell Molly about being magic had pumped up his adrenaline, and now he had all this excess energy to get rid of. Maybe he should go home and grab his skateboard. *Yeah, that would be good*. The air was dry for a change, no snow in sight. Good boarding weather.

He thought about what Molly had said—about being glad to be living today rather than in the past. But he kind of wished he *did* live in the past. *Oh, not* too *long ago, not in the days of gas lighting and horse-drawn carriages or anything.* But in the time before he stepped into magic and his whole world changed. Could it only have been a few weeks ago?

Shoving his hands into his pockets, he turned to go home. He had taken only a few steps when something made him stop short on the pavement. The air shimmered in front of him.

Titania, Queen of Faerie, materialized before him. And she didn't look happy.

Chapter Two

Brighton, England

A BOY WITH GRIMY LONG BLOND HAIR stood beside a crowd of kids. The group stared down at a pink chalk hopscotch grid the boy had drawn on the sidewalk. A little girl, about seven, squinted up at him.

"Does everyone play dress up where you're from?" she asked.

The boy, Daniel, glanced down at his tattered overcoat, patched trousers, and the beat-up top hat he held in his hand. The overcoat with tails had seen better days. It had begun to deteriorate even before he had gone to Free Country. No surprise, seeing as he had found them in the rubbish heap. The trousers had once belonged to one of the sons of his master in the factory. Hand-me-down hand-me-downs they were.

Daniel looked at the neat and tidy children surrounding him and felt a bit disheveled. Usually, he didn't mind how he looked. Everyone in Free Country looked however they wanted to. Well, truth be told, he always made sure his face was clean and nothing was too dirty if he knew he'd be seeing Marya. He was sweet on her, and he didn't care who knew it.

"Where I come from," he told the little girl, "you can dress up as a fairy princess if you want to. Or a frog, even."

The girl giggled. "I wouldn't want to be a frog."

"Well, then, don't, for all I care." Daniel was growing impatient. A dozen children had already hopped the pattern. This batch had slowed things down by asking questions.

"Come on," he instructed them. "Hook it. If you can't hop any faster than this, we'll catch it for sure!"

He watched with satisfaction as the children picked up speed—excited, no doubt, by the possibility of being princesses and frogs. After the last child hopped, skipped, and jumped, Daniel started to follow but paused, teetering on one foot.

"Slag me," he scolded himself. "I forgot! I promised Marya I'd snag her a souvenir."

He placed his bare foot back on the ground

and glanced into the window of the shop behind him. Daniel couldn't read, so he wasn't sure what kind of shop it was. But there was a little statue in the window of a ballerina.

"Coo," he breathed, admiring the statue. "Ain't you the cat's canary." It was just the thing for Marya. He picked up a stone from the gutter and hurled it at the window. Taking care not to cut himself, he reached in and snatched the statue. He shoved it under his coat and hopped his way back home into Free Country.

A moment later, Daniel stood on a cobble-stone path in Free Country, surrounded on all sides by trees, flowers, and rolling lawns. The sun warmed the stones so they felt cozy under his bare feet. The sky was the same brilliant blue it always was, and a hint of the smell of chocolate cookies was in the breeze. Daniel took a deep breath, filling his lungs with the delicious air. "Free Country," he murmured, "and about time, too. Another day of that drudge and I'd have been Bedlam bait."

How long was I out there on my mission? he wondered. It was probably only about three days, but it had felt like years. That's how passing time felt to Daniel anyplace but in Free Country. When he was anywhere else he felt all nervous.

His charges—the children he had just

instructed in the special hopscotch pattern—stood gazing about them. *They all look a bit daft when they come through*, he observed. *Well, no mind. They'll get themselves sorted soon enough. And meantime, I've got a present to give!* He patted the ballerina statue under his coat. He couldn't wait to see Marya's face when he gave it to her.

He pushed his way through the crowd of confused children. "Coming through, coming through," he bleated. He charged up the hill, where some of the children Daniel had sent through earlier were gathered around Kerwyn.

Kerwyn was tall and skinny, and whenever he spoke to the newcomers, he made his voice deeper and lower than it really was. Why he'd want to sound like an old 'un was something Daniel didn't understand. *Isn't that why we're all here? To get away from the grown-ups?*

Daniel thought Kerwyn would sound more commanding if he didn't use all those *ahems*, *ers*, and *uhms*, when he spoke. *Blimey, Kerwyn's given the same speech a million times, so why does he still sound like he's trying to guess at what he wants to say?*

Okay, maybe a million is an exaggeration, Daniel conceded. Daniel wasn't really sure how long Kerwyn had been here. He knew it was a lot longer than him. Or Marya. Maybe longer than everyone. That was one of the reasons Kerwyn was head boy. That, and the fact that at fourteen years old, he was the oldest among them. And always had been. And always would be.

"Ahem," Kerwyn cleared his throat. "I am sure you all, ahem, have questions about . . . uh . . . er . . . things."

Daniel tried not to laugh. Not a single child was paying the least bit of attention to Kerwyn. Maybe the kiddies should have had some questions, but they were having too much fun, discovering the amazing pleasures of Free Country. Boys and girls were rolling down the soft sweet grassy hills. Others chased brightly colored butterflies, who obliged by landing on their noses, tickling them between their astonished eyes. One group was plucking the candy lollipops that sometimes sprang right out of the ground.

"If I could have your attention, please?" Kerwyn asked. Now his voice was back to his ordinary pitch, which was sort of whiney.

"Kerwyn," Daniel said.

Kerwyn looked annoyed. "I didn't mean you, Daniel. I meant the new ones."

"Where's Marya?" Daniel asked.

Kerwyn crossed his arms over his chest. He wore a white shirt, with poofy sleeves that dangled a little along his wrists. Marya called it a "poet's shirt." But as far as Daniel knew, Kerwyn never

made up any of that kind of soppy poetry stuff.
Kerwyn much preferred spending his time making
speeches and playing word games.

"Really," Kerwyn said, rolling his dark eyes.
"That is a stupid question. How should I know
where Marya is?"

Daniel glared at Kerwyn, feeling anger rising.
Did Kerwyn not want him to see Marya? He glared
at the taller boy and advanced a step.

Kerwyn took a tiny step backward. "Out
mooning with the Shimmers, I suppose." Kerwyn
threw up his hands. "Isn't she always?"

Of course! Whenever Daniel didn't know
Marya's whereabouts, he could always find her
with the Shimmers.

"Thanks, mate!" Daniel called over his shoulder as he dashed away.

He charged down to the clear and cold river,
which was full of rainbow fish leaping out of the
water to greet him. "No time to play now," he told
a speckled bass.

He hopped onto his lovely, handmade raft.
Daniel was quite pleased with his accomplishment,
and that made him protective of it. He never let
anyone but Marya ride on his raft. Before he came
to Free Country, Daniel had never owned anything
that was *only* his. Working in the filthy, noisy,
stifling factory, anything he'd made had belonged to

his master, Slaggingham. Everything there, by rights, was his master's: Daniel's time, even his life, it sometimes felt. But this raft, this was *his*.

Grabbing the tree branch that he used as a pole, he guided the raft downriver. To Marya.

Gliding downstream, he grinned, knowing he'd soon be seeing her. He knew exactly where to find the Shimmers. They danced in a little pool overhung with willow trees, just where the sun usually set.

The Shimmers are pretty, Daniel supposed. But he didn't really understand why Marya spent so much time with them. They were hardly even real. *You can practically see through them. Marya is far prettier than any of that lot.* But girls like shiny little things, and the Shimmers were certainly that.

He finally spotted her in the distance, sitting on an overturned rowboat. She was a little slip of a thing, really, and just about his age—thirteen— with beautiful long red hair that curled and danced in the breeze. Her skin was pale white, like those dolls that have glass heads, and her eyes were the most sparkly green. Greener even than the greenest grass of Free Country—and that was the greenest Daniel had ever seen. There hadn't been too much green in Daniel's world. In fact, where Daniel had come from, there was very little that wasn't covered with soot and grime.

Marya was so clean. He liked that, too.

Daniel ducked his hand into the river and gave his face a scrub. He ran his wet hand through his blond hair, hoping it wasn't too much of a mess. Kerwyn did sometimes scold him for being so untidy. Usually Daniel felt like clocking Kerwyn for that. But sometimes he thought perhaps Kerwyn was just trying to help him along a bit. To fit in, like. Make a good impression.

Daniel poled up into the tall grasses of the riverbank. Without his asking, the grass parted for him, so that he could maneuver the raft into place. The long green fronds knew he was in a hurry. Free Country was like that sometimes. You just wanted something and before you'd really realized that you'd made a wish, Free Country gave it to you. It didn't always happen that way, though. Daniel wished and wished for Marya to kiss him and she never did. Not even once. He was still puzzling over why Free Country gave him some things but not what he wanted most.

He leaped onto the bank and hurried toward Marya.

"Marya," he called. "I'm back!" He wondered if she had missed him. Maybe he'd impress her with how many of the little kiddies he had brought back.

"I've done it!" he boasted as he made his way to her through the long grass. "We reeled in the lot of 'em."

He clambered onto the overturned boat that Marya sat on and sprawled beside her. "You ought to see the world they's from," he told her. "They got these boxes they string to their ears that makes music and games like you never seen."

Marya nodded a little, and she gave a small smile so Daniel knew she had noticed he was there. That was a start, at least.

"There'll be more of 'em scarping over any time now," he continued. "Kerwyn'll be picking missionaries for the last crossing soon as he gets the new ones tucked away."

"That's good," Marya murmured.

Daniel laughed. "You don't give a fig, do you? Not really."

Now Marya gave a real smile, even though she still didn't look at him. "No," she answered. "I don't."

Daniel tore his eyes away from Marya's pretty face and followed her gaze. The Shimmers were putting on a splendid show.

He wasn't sure exactly what they were. They looked like little cherubs, only they weren't chubby. They were silvery and pink and glowing, and the air around wherever they were glowed, too. They didn't touch the ground but floated above the river, dancing. They were always dancing. Daniel had to admit they were very impressive—all fluttery and floaty like that. Marya always said they were the most delicate, graceful dancers she'd ever seen. Daniel had never seen any other dancers so he took her word for it.

He stood up and dug his bare toes into the soft wet riverbank. "I don't care about that stuff, neither," he told Marya. "It was fun, being picked for the mission and all, but after that . . ."

He glanced over his shoulder. He was going to tell Marya something he had never said out loud to anyone. "It weren't so bad over there, you know. Not so bad as Kerwyn says. The air weren't that bad. It was a sight better than where I came from. The water, too." He thrust out his bottom lip as he thought about things. "And only a few of the little 'uns looked like they was getting the stick at all regular." He shook his head. "That Kerwyn. He's such a jerk."

Marya didn't respond—not even to this bold statement. She just stared at the Shimmers. He'd never get her attention with them about. He would have tried running them off, but this was their spot. He figured they'd never go.

He sighed and flopped back down onto the rowboat. Maybe if he tried harder to care about the Shimmers, he'd be able to spend more time with Marya. He sat silently beside her, watching the fancy creatures dance their fancy patterns. They were kind of mesmerizing. Still, Marya outshone even their glowing presence.

"You ever try dancing with 'em?" he asked.

Marya finally gazed straight at Daniel. It made his heart feel all gooshy. "Dance with them?" she repeated. "How could I? Look at them."

He watched them for a few more seconds. Marya could do anything, he was sure of it. Why didn't she see that?

"Oh, just you wait," he assured her. "You're bound to catch on sooner or later. Besides, they've been here a long time. A real long time."

Marya's shoulders slumped. "So have I," she mumbled. "Only I never grow up. I just stay the same."

"Who'd want to grow up?" Daniel said. "Not me!"

Marya stared down at her feet. Her long hair covered her face, but Daniel could tell that she'd gone all quiet inside again.

Now you've gone and done it, Daniel scolded himself. He forgot that Marya wasn't always happy to be in Free Country. And that she'd probably been trying to dance like the Shimmers as long as

she'd been here. "Snaffle me, Marya. I'm sorry."
Do something, he told himself. *Make it better.*

He sat back up and felt the weight in his
inside coat pocket. *Perfect!* "Never mind that," he
said, pulling out the ballerina statue. "Look, I
brought you something." He handed Marya the
dancing girl. She stared down at it, her green eyes
wide.

His stomach felt suddenly sick. She was supposed to smile when he gave her the doll. "What's
the matter?" he asked. "I thought you'd like it.
You're always thinking about the old palace days
and learning to be a ballerina and all."

"I do like it. I do," Marya told him.

Girls are funny, Daniel thought. *Marya's lips
are smiling, but her eyes are still sad.*

"She's beautiful. I promise I like it," Marya
assured him. As if to prove it, she kissed the
statue's head and looked up at Daniel.

Daniel wished she had kissed him instead. It
made him want to smash the stupid statue. He
shoved his hands into his overcoat pockets.

She still didn't seem ready to leave the
Shimmers, so he lay back down beside her. At
least now, though, she was looking at the statue
he'd given her instead of at the shining dancers
above the pool.

"Tell me what it was like," Daniel asked her,

"in that Petersburg place of yours."

"I've told you a dozen times," Marya protested.

"But I like hearing the telling," he said. What he truly liked was the excuse to stay close to Marya. He liked having her tell him stories about her life.

Marya gave a little smile and lay the statue across her lap. "Once, long, long ago, my mother belonged to the Empress."

"Belonged?" Daniel repeated. Marya had never started the story quite like that before—never used the word "belonged." "Like that statue I just gave you belongs to you?"

"Yes, exactly like that."

"I wouldn't want to belong to nobody!" Daniel said.

"It didn't seem strange at the time," Marya said. "It was just the way it was. And Mama got to wear pretty dresses, and I did, too, and eat well and live in the palace year-round."

"That part would have been all right." Daniel had spent most of his thirteen years sweating by the coal furnaces of the factory or freezing while scrounging for food or shelter.

"Yes," Marya said in her soft voice. "But Mama had to do whatever the Empress wanted. They all did. So when the Empress went to France one day and saw people dance a way she liked, she came back and told all her servants to bring her their girl children."

"No boys?" Daniel always asked that question in the same spot in the story.

Marya smiled. "No boys. My mother had to make me go. I didn't want to. The Empress scared me."

"She scares me, too." Daniel shivered.

"The Empress looked at all the girls and she picked the prettiest ones."

"So of course she picked you!" Daniel always said this, too.

Marya stood and pointed at Daniel. "You are going to dance for me!" she said in a highfalutin, bossy tone.

She jumped off the boat and sat cross-legged on the grass. Daniel flopped down and stretched out beside her. The Free Country grass came together under him to form a pillow.

"If the Empress picked you, you couldn't be with your family very much," Marya continued. "You spent too much time practicing ways to stand and move. If you didn't catch on, they'd hit your legs with a stick. They gave you shoes that had wood on the toes. The dancing shoes made your feet bleed."

"It weren't right!" Daniel was furious at Marya's mistreatment. He hated the shoes that crushed her toes and made them bleed, the dancing master who beat the students. "I'd 'uv flung those biting shoes straight at that dancing fool's head!"

"But I wanted to dance!" Marya exclaimed. "It wasn't all bad. There was something in the dance that was good—like a promise."

She pulled her knees up to her chest and wrapped her slim pale arms around them. Her eyes looked dreamy. "Sometimes you'd feel like you could soar away from everything—just glide, free, if only you knew how." She tilted her head and looked at Daniel. It made him turn shy—her gaze was so direct for once. "I thought it might make a difference if I took off the shoes. And it did. A little bit. But not enough. It wasn't the shoes that held me down. It was that I had never learned how to fly. No one else knew either. No one could show me how."

Daniel's eyes went to the Shimmers. He was finally understanding why Marya was always here. "The Shimmers fly, don't they?" he asked. "They know."

"Yes, they do. But I don't think they can teach me. It's their own dance." She faced the Shimmers again. "I think everyone must have to find her own dance."

She had never said so much before. Daniel

reached over and gripped her hands. "What do you think your dance would be?"

He must have grabbed her small, cool hands too tightly, because she winced. He instantly released her soft fingers.

Daniel stared at the dirt, ashamed. "I'm sorry," he mumbled.

"I know," Marya replied.

They sat quietly for a few minutes. He couldn't help her, and it made him sad and a little bit angry.

"Did you say that Kerwyn will be choosing the next missionary?" Marya asked.

"Any time now," Daniel said. Was she hoping that he would go, go away? She wanted to be rid of him, didn't she? He couldn't bear to look at her in case that was what she was thinking.

Marya stood, clutching the statue. "Thank you for the dance," she said to the Shimmers. "And for my present," she said to Daniel. And then she ran off, leaving him alone.

Chapter Three

Tim STARED, TRYING to grasp the implications of what he was seeing.

Titania stood there, clear as day, on the sidewalk in a run-down section of London. She looked wildly out of place—her pale green skin was only one of the attributes that made her stand out.

For another thing, she was spectacularly beautiful. Even her weird green skin didn't detract from her beauty. Tim could not have said exactly what it was that made her more beautiful than anyone he'd ever seen. Maybe it had something to do with the fact that she was filled with magic.

Her long hair was dark green, and today it was woven through with tiny flowers. She wore a flowing silver gown that shimmered whenever she moved. Her long sleeves were pale, transparent blue—the color of twilight. She had large, almond-shaped eyes that changed color with her mood. They were a deep purple now, and Tim felt their furious glare as if she were actually touching him. He took several steps backward.

"How dare you?" she shrieked. "You terrible, foolish child."

Tim clenched his jaw. "How dare I what? Risk my life to save your world? I suppose a thank-you is too much to ask for."

Titania took a step toward him and Tim forced himself to stay put. He felt a cold draft emanating from her and he shivered.

"You are insolent," she growled. "No one speaks to me in that manner."

Tim's brown eyes never wavered from hers. After all, what he had said was true: He *had* saved Faerie and it had cost him plenty. She ought to be thanking him, not shouting at him. But he had discovered that adults didn't always behave in any normal or rational way.

Titania made a slow circle around Tim, as if she were studying a specimen. Tim took the opportunity to glance around. No one on the street seemed to have noticed her. *Do they think I'm speaking to myself?* he wondered. *Or has she cloaked us both in some invisibility spell? She could probably do something like that easily enough.*

Titania stopped in front of him again. "It was not only love he spurned for your sake but life as well. You have been the death of your father."

Tim's head snapped back as if she had struck him. The words stung. "Don't you think I know that?" he shouted. "I live with that every minute of the day."

A nasty smile spread across Titania's face. "Well, at least you suffer," she said.

"Did you ever think maybe he sacrificed himself so he wouldn't have to be trapped in a world with you any longer?" Tim retorted.

Now Titania looked wounded, as if Tim's words had the prick of truth in them. She quickly recovered. "You do your father no honor, changeling," she spat at him. "Had you an ounce of skill, you would not have needed such a sacrifice from him. You walked blindly into that lair. You know nothing, and your ignorance is your curse. You are not just a fool, you are dangerous."

Tim was not going to let this horrid woman get the best of him. "Are you quite finished yelling at me? I really have to be going now."

"Go where you will, Timothy Hunter," Titania said, her voice nearly a growl. "Prowl these gray and dingy streets or sink all the way to Hell. But go knowing what you are: a cursed fool."

Fury and pain made Timothy brave—or at least bold. "Oh, I know what I am all right, your royal bitchiness," he declared. He jerked a thumb toward himself. "I'm the fool that saved *you* and your world—and lost a father for my troubles. You would be dead without me. You *owe* me. Live with that!"

Without a backward glance, Tim spun around and left the Queen of Faerie standing on the London sidewalk. He forced himself not to look back, to keep moving forward, to move as if he had some idea of where he might be going. He didn't even care if she followed him, or sent gremlins on his trail or whatever the Queen of Faerie might do when raving. He didn't care about anything at all. She was right about one thing: His father was dead—and it was all his fault.

He found himself in a familiar location—the cemetery.

Everything had gotten so confusing after his mother died; everything had changed. He missed his mum so much, but he never felt like he had anyplace to express it. He was always worried about his dad's—Mr. Hunter's—feelings. Mr. Hunter already blamed himself for Tim's mother's death, for not being the one to die. He was completely adrift without her. How could Tim add his own loss to that? So Tim had hidden his hurt and kept things to himself.

Tim took the familiar winding path until he

came to his mother's grave. He sank down beside the gravestone and leaned his head against it, feeling its hard coolness.

Tim noticed scrawny little weeds poking skinny shoots up out of the dirt covering his mum's grave. "What are these?" he muttered. He reached to pluck the pathetic-looking things. Then his hand froze as he remembered.

When Tim had been dying in Faerie, he had been whisked out of his body by a pretty young woman who just happened to be the incarnation of Death. They had a long talk, and when Tim woke up back inside his body, he had found a packet of seeds in his pocket. A packet he had seen Death find in her messy apartment. When Tim returned to his own world, he had visited his mum's grave and planted the seeds.

The infant plants didn't look like much, but Tim knew that appearances could be deceiving. Besides, he figured seeds given to him by Death herself must be pretty important. She'd gone through a lot of trouble to find them. It would probably be a bad idea to pull them up. Better to wait and see what they turned out to be.

Tim stood up stiffly. Sometimes he felt better after visiting his mum's grave. Not today, though. Today, he felt weighed down by Titania's words. He had tried to drown them out, but they hit too close to home. He had caused Tamlin's death, and there was no way he could argue himself out of that one. And she was right about his ignorance— it made him dangerous. But then why didn't anyone teach him anything? It made no sense that the Trenchcoat Brigade would dump this ability into his lap without an instruction manual.

No, nothing made sense to Tim. Least of all the adults who seemed to be bent on ripping his reality to shreds.

Chapter Four

MARYA CRADLED THE BALLERINA statue in her arms as she hurried to her tent. The conversation with Daniel had unsettled her.

He needs so much, she thought. She felt bad but she knew his need was a bottomless pit, and nothing she said or did could ever fill it.

There was something else, too. She felt she had finally hit upon a truth when she talked to him about the Shimmers. They couldn't teach her what she needed to know. Only *she* could discover how to dance in the way she wanted to.

She could pirouette, and pose in arabesque, and plié, but couldn't use the movement to express what she was feeling inside. She could do the steps, make the patterns, but she couldn't move with the transporting, compelling grace of a Shimmer. What she had realized while talking to Daniel was that dancing should be about what was inside her, not what her muscles and limbs could do. That was the difference between her and the Shimmers. They were at peace; they lived in harmony with their surroundings. Their insides and their outsides were one.

That was what Marya had to learn to do.

She entered her tent, which Daniel had helped her set up a long time ago. It was really just sheets slung over the branches of several trees, clipped together so that they wouldn't slip. Marya had decorated the branches with chiffon scarves and flower garlands. A trunk held all of her belongings—of which she had few. She stored the various presents that Daniel had given her in the trunk, too. She slept on the soft grass and used a tree stump as a table. She liked being able to watch how the sun changed the colors inside the tent as it filtered through the different layers of fabric.

She placed the little ballerina statue on the tree stump and lay down on the grass, her arms under her head as she formulated a plan.

After a short time, she stood and stretched. She knew what she needed to do. First things first. She left her tent and located Kerwyn, making sure he didn't see her. She hid behind a thick tree and watched him for a few minutes. He was surrounded by a group of children, probably the new ones Daniel had brought in. Kerwyn should be busy for a little longer.

Next, she went to Kerwyn's cave. She never understood why he would choose to live underground. Marya's tent was light and airy, while Kerwyn's shelter was dark and dank. But Free Country gave each child what they needed, so maybe the dark made Kerwyn feel protected and safe. Marya knew a bit of what Kerwyn had gone through on that Crusade. The cave must let him feel hidden. Had Marya undergone such an ordeal, she might want to hide, too.

Marya looked around the small cavern. Candles stood in niches carved into the rock walls. Books were strewn about everywhere. Bags of chalk sat in one corner. None of these was what she was looking for.

Her green eyes lit on a stack of board games. Kerwyn could spend hours playing these games. Several of the children from later times had brought them through, often losing interest in them once they discovered all the activities Free Country offered. They abandoned them for swimming and tumbling and rafting and playing dress up. Kerwyn then inherited the games, and he loved them. He didn't care if there were no other players. Sometimes he'd sit and play all sides. Both the white and the black checkers, the hat and the car and the iron in Monopoly.

His favorite, though, far above the rest, was the word game. He would set up four sets of tiles, and make words appear all over the board. He kept a dictionary at hand, and once Marya had heard him arguing with himself over whether or not a word was admissible for points. It grew quite heated, with Kerwyn arguing both sides. Apparently something called "triple bonus points" were at stake.

Marya opened the box and took all the little tiles with the letters on them. She slipped them into the pocket of her dress. They clicked against each other as she hurried back to the hill where she'd last seen Kerwyn.

Kerwyn was alone now, sitting with his back against a tree, gazing out over Free Country. He was watching the new children exploring their freedom.

Marya climbed the hill and stood over Kerwyn. "Kerwyn? Listen. I'm ready," she said.

"What?" Kerwyn glanced up at her.

"I'm ready. I want to go on the next mission."

"That's silly. You're a girl." Kerwyn went back to watching the little ones. A small girl was picking flowers that instantly replaced themselves the moment the first ones were plucked from the ground.

"What does that have to do with anything?" Marya demanded. She hated it when Kerwyn said stupid things like that.

"Our group has only one assignment left, and it's important." Kerwyn sounded as if he were a very old man explaining things to a very young— and slow—girl. Daniel was right. What was the word that he had used? Kerwyn was a jerk.

"This is probably the most important mission anyone's got. And you are a girl." He stood up. Marya knew that as far as he was concerned, the conversation was over.

Only it wasn't. Far from it.

"Kerwyn? You like to play that word game, don't you? Scribble?"

"Scrabble. Yes . . ." Now he looked confused.

"Well, someone's taken all the pieces. Those square letter things? And hidden them." She laughed. "To tell the truth, I did it." She pirouetted, then grinned at him. "I'll bet you'd do just about anything to get them back, wouldn't you?"

Kerwyn leaped to his feet. "Do you think I'd jeopardize the whole mission just to—"

"Of course you would," Marya cut him off with another laugh. "Anyone sensible would."

Kerwyn stared at her. "You evil brat!"

She wasn't upset by his calling her names. She knew he didn't really mean it. It was simply the proof that she'd won.

"Maybe I am and maybe I'm not," she said. "But I know how to get things done, don't I?" She'd been right. He loved the Scrabble enough that he'd do anything to get his pieces back. Even send a mere girl on a mission.

Kerwyn paced a few minutes. Finally he stopped and glared at her. "All right. Since you're so clever. How's this for fair? You get to go. You can go on this mission. But if you fail, you can't come back here. Ever."

That didn't scare her one bit. "I'll go pack right now!"

She hurried back to her tent, trying to figure out what she should bring with her. She slung a cloth pouch over her shoulder and looked around her little space.

"Hmmm. Chalk!" She bent down and put the colored chalk into her pouch. That was a definite. "Her." She picked up the ballerina statue, smiled at it, then slipped it into the pouch. "Apples." She might get hungry. "Comb. Bracelet." She glanced around her tent, pondering. "More apples?"

Daniel popped his head through the opening of the tent.

"You done it!" he exclaimed. "You got 'round Kerwyn! He hardly ever lets the girls do anything!"

"Uh-huh." She waved him to come in, then

knelt by the trunk, wondering if she'd forgotten anything.

Daniel squatted down beside her. "How'd you ever do it? No one gets 'round Kerwyn."

"Simple. I scared him." She moved some scarves aside, rummaging deeper in the trunk.

"Did you? I wish I could have seen that." Daniel sank back onto his heels and grinned.

"What you got in that bag there? Apples?"

"And my comb and my bracelet. And your present." She lifted the ballerina from the bag to show him.

Daniel's blue eyes widened and he quickly glanced down at the ground, blushing. "I'm glad you're taking something to remember me by."

She smiled. She was glad she had decided to take the statue. It pleased Daniel so much to know she liked it. Daniel tugged at the pouch. "What else you got in there?"

"Uhm, the chalk."

"Well, that's good. Wouldn't get far if you forgot that. Anything else?"

Marya hesitated a moment and then reached down and pulled out a battered pair of dancing shoes. She had never shown them to anyone in Free Country before.

She dangled the ragged pink satin slippers from their fraying pink ribbon, letting them

twirl in front of her face. It had been some time
since she'd taken them out of the trunk. But there
they were in front of her face. Same wood blocks
in the toes. Blood still staining the insides. "Yes,"
she whispered. "I'm taking these."

Daniel looked from her to the shoes, then back
to her face again. She could tell he was unsure what
to say, but she liked the fact that he clearly understood how important the ballet slippers were to her.
He just nodded, then said, "So you're all set then."

"All set. Oh! Except for these." She dropped
the Scrabble tiles onto the tree stump. "Tell
Kerwyn where they are after I've gone."

"All right."

Daniel walked her to the special spot where
the pattern would work. He had to leave her at
the clearing—one could only go through the gate
alone.

She knelt down and drew the hopscotch grid.
Then she turned and waved good-bye. He looked
so sad, but when he realized she was looking at
him, a grin spread across his face. "See ya!" he
called. "Come back soon!"

Marya patted her pouch. She took a deep
breath and began to hop and chant.

"Mary, Mary, quite contrary
How does your garden grow?

With silver bells and cockleshells
And pretty maids all in a row.
My mother says to pick just one
So out goes Y-O-U!"

With that last phrase, she hopped the last
part of the pattern— right out of Free Country.

Chapter Five

TIM STOOD UP AND LOOKED AROUND. There were more people in the cemetery now. On the weekends, the dead always had more visitors.

Tim brushed off his jeans and started walking. It wasn't that he had any destination in mind. *Unless there is some weird realm I haven't yet visited called Explanations Land, or Confusion's End*, Tim mused.

He left the graveyard, and it finally occurred to him that having Titania, Queen of Faerie, as an enemy might not be very good. In fact, antagonizing her the way he had probably wasn't the brightest tack to take. But he'd taken it. There was no going back now.

But he couldn't go forward either. Titania's accusations stung. Mostly because he was so afraid they were true. She was right—he didn't know anything, and that made him dangerous. He hadn't meant to go to the manticore's lair. But if he hadn't, Faerie would still be a wasteland, and Tamlin might have wound up dead anyway. Titania, too, for that matter. Why didn't she see that? He shook his head. *Who knows how her twisted green mind works?*

Grown-ups were always interfering, getting in his way, or plain old coming after him. Still, he supposed he had to try to figure them out—if only in self-defense.

He wandered into a playground and was surprised to see how deserted it was. The only kid around was a chubby girl, about ten years old, sitting on a swing. She rocked slowly back and forth, one foot trailing in the dirt.

This is *Saturday, isn't it?* Tim thought. The place should have been overrun with kids.

The lone girl sat muttering and scowling. Her mood matched Tim's exactly. He sat on the swing beside hers. She glanced over at him.

"Who are you?" she demanded. "Are you one of the kidnappers?"

Kidnappers? Tim raised his eyebrows above his spectacles. He didn't think he particularly looked like a kidnapper. Then again, he didn't exactly look like a magician either, and he supposedly was one. "No. I'm just me. Wondering if you're okay."

"Oh." She looked puzzled. "No one has been asking *me* that." She pouted and kicked her legs hard, setting herself swinging. "They're all too busy worrying about Oliver."

"Who's Oliver?" Tim asked. "And why's everyone so worried about him? Is he sick?"

"No, he's gone missing. Like the others."

"What others?" Tim asked.

She stared at him with open eyes and mouth. "Don't you read the papers? Or watch the news?" She shook her head as if she couldn't believe Tim's sheer stupidity. "I was interviewed on the nine o'clock news after it happened. Mummy taped it and everything."

Tim squinted. The girl's story was beginning to sound familiar. *Of course.* Molly had mentioned missing children earlier that day. But that was in some other town, not here, he thought.

"Didn't that happen somewhere else?"

She rolled her eyes. "First, Brighton. Then here."

That must explain why the playground is empty, Tim thought. *All the children in this neighborhood must have gone missing, too.*

"So," Tim continued, "who is Oliver?"

The girl scowled. "My little brother."

Hm. Clearly she isn't a fan. "So, if all the other kids are gone, why aren't *you* missing?" Tim asked.

"I had to go to the orthodontist." She grimaced and showed him her braces. "When I got home, everyone was gone."

"Do you have any idea where they went?" Tim asked, curious in spite of himself. It was kind of a relief to worry about someone else's problems for a change.

"No one knows. But I bet it has something to do with that foreign kid who was always playing at the abandoned manor."

"What foreign kid?"

"He had a funny accent and wore the strangest clothes. I never saw anyone like him before."

"Where was he from?" Tim asked.

The girl shrugged. "America, I suppose. He kept going on about it being a free country where he came from. Isn't that what they call America? He was always trying to get us to play games. Baby stuff. Hopscotch and the like. Nursery rhymes."

"Have the police been 'round?"

The girl rolled her eyes. "Course they have. Just like on the telly. They asked me loads of questions. But I don't think they'll ever find Oliver."

"Do you miss him?" Tim had always wondered what it would be like to have a sister or brother, especially in the last few weeks when everything had grown more and more confusing.

"My mum does. She's frantic. I wish I was the one missing. No one pays any attention to me. All they care about is my stupid, piggy brother."

So much for sisterly love, Tim thought.

"The foreign kid is gone now, too. Maybe he wasn't behind it at all. Maybe the kidnappers got him as well." The girl shivered. "Maybe someone is out to kidnap all the children in the whole world. I overheard my parents talking, and they said forty children disappeared from Brighton. The same sort of case."

"They'll figure it out, I'm sure," Tim said.

"How do you know?" she demanded in an accusing tone. "You don't know anything."

"Well, what I mean to say is, uhm, I'm sure your brother is okay," Tim said.

"Maybe he is and maybe he isn't."

Tim shook his head. No matter what he tried to say, it was the wrong thing. *Is it me? Is it girls? Is it this girl in particular?* He wasn't even sure which she was more upset about—that her brother had gone missing or that she hadn't.

A woman with light brown hair and wire-rim glasses rushed into the playground. "Avril!" she cried. "You were supposed to be home ten minutes ago! I was so worried."

Ten minutes? My dad doesn't start to worry until I've been gone extra hours, not extra minutes. If then.

The woman charged over to the swing and swooped the girl up into her arms. "I was afraid you'd been stolen away, too," she said.

Tim noticed a smirk cross Avril's face. He suspected that she had planned this. Tim was fairly certain Avril was going to continue being late as long as she could get away with it. She obviously relished the attention.

The woman finally noticed Tim. "You should get home right away, young man," she scolded him. "Go inside and stay there. There are crazy people around."

Tim stood. "You have no idea," he replied.

Marya stood in a confusing jumble of noise and motion. She blinked a few times and took a deep breath. That set her to coughing. The air was gray here, almost chewy, compared to the bright clean world of Free Country.

Where are they all going, she wondered, *and why are they all in such a hurry?* Women in slim short skirts with matching jackets strode purposefully toward stairs that descended underground. Men hurried along carrying newspapers and leather cases.

Daniel was right—people had little boxes

attached to their ears with wires. Others spoke loudly into small devices they held up to their heads.

Marya had seen a city before, though she'd been in Free Country for so long that she wasn't accustomed to such bustle any longer. But this city was nothing like St. Petersburg or any other city she'd seen before. The fountain in the center of the square and the cobblestone side streets reminded her a bit of her old home, but everything was crowded and close together. And there were so many people.

And those vehicles! Where were the horses and the carriages? Strange-looking metal carriages with rubber wheels growled and squealed around her. People shouted at one another from windows of the cars and on the street. It was overwhelming.

Marya took a few steps backward into the protective shadows between two towering shiny buildings.

"Lissen you," a gruff voice growled at her. "Get offer me 'ouse."

Startled, Marya glanced around but saw no one.

"Get off!" the voice shouted.

Marya realized the voice was coming from below her. A head suddenly poked out of the large cardboard box behind her, like a turtle emerging from its shell.

"This is my 'ouse, and I'll have none of yer lot running me out," the man snarled.

Marya stepped off the cardboard flap she'd been standing on. "I'm sorry," she said. "I didn't realize."

The man squinted at her as if he were trying to decide if she were sincere in her apology. His thick face was covered in stubble and dirt.

What kind of world is this? Marya reached into her pouch and pulled out one of her apples to give him. She must have been more nervous than she realized—the apple fell from her hands.

The man stared at the apple, then at Marya, then back at the apple again. With the quickness of a striking cobra, the man snatched the apple. He pulled himself completely inside the box.

"Breakfast?" the man muttered inside his strange little house. "Lunch?" Marya heard a crunching sound: The man must have taken a bite of the apple. "Brunch!"

Satisfied that the man no longer deemed her a house thief, Marya went on her way.

"Timothy Hunter, come out, come out, wherever you are," she chanted in a singsong voice. Her bare feet made no sound on the pavement. She took care to avoid the stickiest, dirtiest spots. Now that she was here, she wasn't quite certain how to begin her mission.

After the first shock of the chaos had worn off, Marya could see why this place had fascinated Daniel. The shop windows were full of such amazing things. She couldn't imagine what they were for or what they did. The people looked so interesting, their faces displaying every conceivable emotion, their clothing clashing in wild disharmony. There was so much movement, so much to see.

Marya watched an unlikely pair of women cross a street. One wore thick, dark face paint, with black rings around her eyes. Tattoos covered the bare arms revealed by her black sleeveless shirt. Next to her was a woman dressed in bright colors, her blond curls pulled into a bouncy tail on top of her head. What struck Marya most was that the woman in black had a big smile on her face and the perky-looking one was scowling angrily. As they crossed to the other side, a young man on a wheeled board veered between them. And a man with exposed knees, white socks, and sandals nearly backed into them as he held a small device in front of his eyes and clicked, pointing the box at a tall building.

"It's like a dance," Marya exclaimed. Somehow all the dancers managed to keep to the imperceptible pattern and not smash into each other.

A sparkling display caught her eye. She stopped to peer into the window of a jewelry store. Bracelets and necklaces sat in velvet cases, glittering in the afternoon light.

This might be just the place, Marya decided. Fixing her bracelet was one of the tasks she had been determined to accomplish in her time away from Free Country.

She opened the door and stepped inside. A little bell jangled, announcing her presence. The store was quiet and clean.

A stout man looked up when he heard the bell. He held a case of gold rings that he was just returning to the glass cabinet. He slipped the case onto a shelf and turned the key in the lock.

He eyed Marya, and she realized it might be unusual to be barefoot in the city. She awkwardly stood with one foot on top of the other, trying to cover up the worst of the dirt.

"Yes, miss?" the man said.

"Do you fix things?" Marya asked.

"We've been known to. If it's jewelry you're talking about."

Marya smiled. "Good." She pulled her precious bracelet from her pouch. "Can you fix this?" She held the bracelet out to the man.

He squinted at it. "Possibly, possibly." He

took the bracelet from her. His hand felt warm and clammy.

"Mmm." He turned the bracelet over, then held it up to the light. His squinty eyes opened wide. "Good lord!" he exclaimed. "A Lermontov!"

His hand closed around the bracelet. Marya didn't like the way it disappeared into his fat hand.

He leaned over the counter and glared at her. "All right, young woman. Where did you steal this?"

Shocked by the accusation, Marya replied indignantly, "My mother gave it to me! Empress Anna gave it to her. But it didn't fit her right so she gave it to me." There. That should settle things. She rummaged in her pouch and brought out an apple. It was shiny and perfect. "Will you fix it? I'll give you an apple."

"An apple?" the man bellowed. He leaned over the counter even farther. His face was mere inches from Marya's. His breath was stale. "Off with you this instant! And be glad I don't have you arrested." He pointed sternly toward the door.

Marya stared back at him. Why did her bracelet make him so angry? She looked at the apple. *It's a particularly nice apple*, she thought, *the best of the lot. Maybe I should have offered two?*

The man came out from behind the counter,

placed a meaty hand on Marya's slight shoulder, and practically shoved her out the door. "Go! And don't let me see you here again, or I shall call the police on you!"

The door slammed behind her.

"But . . . my bracelet . . ." she protested meekly. Marya had been in Free Country for an awfully long time. It had been ages since anyone had treated her so roughly. She wasn't sure how to respond.

Feeling defeated and forlorn, she leaned against one of the potted plants that stood on either side of the jewelry store door. "My mother gave it to me," she murmured. She traced a pattern on the pavement with her big toe. "It's all I have left . . ." Marya crossed her thin arms over her chest and tried to keep herself from crying.

"What's wrong?" the potted plant asked.

This didn't surprise Marya. In Free Country, that sort of thing happened all the time.

"That store man took my bracelet," Marya explained to the plant. "He said I'd stolen it, then he took it."

An interesting face appeared between the parted fronds of the plant. "Oh, he did, did he?" the person in the plant said.

Marya was pretty sure it was a woman's face. She wore paint on her lips and her eyelids, but her hair was short, even shorter than most of the boys' in Free Country. And it was a purplish black, like the color of a bruise. Marya had never seen anyone with hair that color before. A sparkly jewel glittered in the side of the woman's nose.

"I just wanted the man to fix it," Marya explained, "so I could wear it again. But now it's gone."

The long ferns parted, and now Marya could clearly see that the plant person was a woman, even though her clothing seemed more appropriate for a man. She wore a white button down shirt, a skinny black tie, black pants with black suspenders, and a long white apron. She leaped through the leaves and over the side of the large cement container that held the plant. She dropped a cigarette to the pavement and stubbed it out with her heavy black shoe. "You just stay here," the woman said. "I'll take care of this."

Marya watched as the determined woman pushed open the jewelry store door and stepped inside.

Marya sat down on the cement plant holder and waited. A few minutes later, the woman came out, dangling the bracelet in front of her. "Here you go," the woman said.

Marya had no idea how the woman had done it, but she was thrilled. "Thank you!" she exclaimed, taking it back. The bracelet could stay broken, as long as she never came that close to losing it again.

The woman stretched, then grinned. "No problem."

"Are you a dancer?" Marya asked the woman. "You move like a dancer."

"Me? A dancer?" The woman laughed. "Not even close. Though this waitress gig has me on my feet all day. Spinning and ducking and lifting."

"Oh!" Marya reached into her bag and pulled out an apple. "Would you like an apple? They're very nice."

She held the apple out to the woman. She wanted to give her something as a reward for retrieving her bracelet. She knew that when someone does you a favor you should always show your thanks with a gift. That was the way it was done in the palace. If her mother worked extra hard to be sure the empress's dress had three dozen more feathers on it, the empress would often give her a little gift. Or if her mother delivered a secret message, or sent someone away that the empress wished to avoid, another gift would arrive. Sometimes a gift for Marya would be sent along, too. That was before Marya had been taken away to learn to dance. She never received any gifts after that.

"My name's Annie," the waitress said, eyeing the apple.

"I'm Marya. Really, the apple is quite good," she assured Annie. "It isn't a bit like in Snow White."

Annie laughed. "Believe me, I'd never be mistaken for that gal." She took the apple and bit into it. A huge grin spread across her face and her eyes shut as if she were thinking the nicest thoughts in the world. "Mmmmm. This is delicious." Her eyes popped open. They were a lovely shade of chocolate brown. "I haven't had an apple this good since I was six or seven."

"Why were you in the plant?" Marya asked. After meeting the man who lived in a box, she wondered if the tree was where Annie lived.

"I wasn't in the plant," Annie explained, crunching on the apple. "I was on the other side, sneaking a ciggie. I swore I'd quit, so I didn't want anyone to catch me from the café. I heard you and wanted to find out who it was speaking on the other side."

"Oh."

"I was on a break . . . which is quite over now. Well, it helps to be headwaitress." She gave Marya a once-over, as she took another bite of the apple. A little juice trickled down her chin. She wiped it off and grinned. "For this, I owe you a fizzy drink at least."

Annie lay a hand with painted blue fingernails

on Marya's shoulder. Her hand was calloused and rough, but her touch was light. Not like the clamping paw of the man in the jewelry store.

"All right," Marya said. "But I can't stay long. I have to find somebody."

Annie walked Marya around the plant and opened the door to a cheerful café. Black-and-white linoleum made a checkerboard pattern on the floor. Booths ran along the large windows, and red leather stools with chrome posts sat before a shiny silver counter. One little old lady sat at a booth, nursing a cup of tea. Two boys about Marya's age sat at the counter, sipping tall frosty drinks through straws.

"This place is a lot bigger than I thought it would be," Marya said, settling onto a stool at the very end of the counter.

"What, the café?" Annie asked. She slipped behind the chrome counter and reached below it for a tall glass, which she filled with ice.

"No," Marya replied, "the city."

Annie used a strange hose to fill the glass with liquid. "So you're not from around here, I take it?" Annie gave Marya the glass and popped a straw into it. Marya took a sip of the sweet, bubbly drink.

"No," Marya replied. The bubbles tickled, and her nose wrinkled.

"I should have guessed that from your accent," Annie said, "which is quite lovely, I must say." She leaned against the back counter and took another bite of the apple.

"Thank you. So is yours," Marya said. She liked the rough way the waitress spoke. It made her sound like she had grit in her teeth.

"You're supposed to meet someone here?" Annie asked. "Or near here?"

"Oh no," Marya said, making the high seat swivel. It squeaked a little. "He doesn't know I'm looking for him."

"I know the feeling, luv." Annie laughed. "So give us a hint. How do you propose to find this mystery man?"

Marya held the glass and thought seriously about the question. She realized that she didn't have a plan at all. "I haven't decided yet."

She couldn't fail this mission. No matter what she thought of Kerwyn, Free Country needed help. Besides, if she failed in getting Tim to Free Country, Kerwyn would decide it was because she was a girl, and she didn't like that. Not at all.

"I guess I thought I would just know how to find him once I got here," Marya confessed. She hoped that didn't make her sound foolish.

Annie grinned. "Just as I suspected. You're one of those optimists I keep hearing about." She winked at Marya. "Well, it's a slow shift. Tell you what. For a small commission, I'll see if I can't help you find your gentleman."

Marya could not believe her good fortune. First this kind woman had retrieved her bracelet, and now she was going to help her with her mission. "Oh, that would be wonderful!" Marya's brow furrowed. "What's a commission?"

Annie tossed the apple core into a trash bin. "In this case, another of those apples. If you can spare another, that is."

That seemed fair. Marya solemnly handed over another apple, shining it first on the hem of her dress.

Annie picked up a thick book from the back counter. "Now to business. This mysterious young man of yours. He is young, isn't he?" She plopped the book down in front of Marya.

"Yes. About my age."

"Splendid. And he does have a name, doesn't he?"

Marya giggled. "Of course he does. It's Timothy. Timothy Hunter."

Annie flipped open the book. She turned several of the pages. Marya saw that the pages were filled with long lists of names with numbers beside them.

Annie ran her blue fingernail along one page.

"Figures. There must be a thousand Hunters in here." She glanced at Marya. "You wouldn't know his old man's name, would you? Or his mum's?"

"I don't think he has a mother anymore." Marya bit her lip, trying to remember. "But I think Kerwyn said that his father's name is . . . William."

"Then he'll be a Bill or a Will or a William. There can't be more than forty of them. Piece of cake."

"No, thank you." Marya was too excited about finding Timothy Hunter to eat.

"What?" Annie looked confused for a moment, then she smiled. "Oh. No. It's an expression: piece of cake. It means dead easy."

"Oh."

Annie balanced the book on one arm and plucked a strange-looking device from a holder on the wall. She punched little buttons on it and grinned at Marya. "I'll just phone them all," she promised.

So that must be what that interesting thing is, Marya observed. *A phone. I've heard about them from the children who came to Free Country recently from this world.*

"Hello?" Annie said into the telephone. "Is this the Hunter residence? This sounds odd, I know, but do you happen to have a boy named Timothy? Sorry to trouble you, then. Ta."

She put the phone back into its cradle on the wall, then faced Marya and shrugged. "One down. Thirty-nine to go."

Annie punched number after number. She sometimes had to stop, as people came into the café. Annie chatted up the customers and brought them plates of food. While she did this, Marya held her finger on the line in the phone book so that Annie wouldn't lose her spot in the long column of names and numbers.

What with the frequent breaks, quite a bit of time had passed when they reached the end of the list.

Annie placed a plate in front of Marya. "You must be hungry by now," she said.

Marya stared down at the plate. On it sat two slices of toasted bread, with something yellow and gooey oozing out the sides.

"Go on," Annie encouraged her. "That grilled cheese won't bite."

Marya didn't feel hungry, but she picked up the sandwich anyway and nibbled one corner, without moving her finger from the spot on the page. Annie had gone to the trouble of fixing her this snack. She couldn't be rude and not eat it. Not after Annie had helped her so much.

"Come on. It's not the end of the world," Annie said. She rested her elbows on the counter.

"What's so special about this Tim anyway?"

"He's magic."

Marya could feel Annie's chocolate-colored eyes on her. Had that been the wrong thing to say? But it was the truth. That was what was so special about Timothy Hunter.

Annie stood back up and placed her fists on her hips. "He is, is he?"

Marya snuck a peek at Annie from under her long lashes and saw that she was smiling.

"Well, perhaps we won't give up on him just yet," Annie said. "We've got one last William to try."

Annie turned the directory around so that it faced her. Marya lifted her finger so that Annie could read the number.

Annie punched in numbers again. Marya wished and hoped for luck.

"Hello? Is Timothy Hunter there?" Annie covered the mouthpiece with one hand. Her brown eyes twinkled. "We've got it!" she exclaimed. Then she lowered her voice and added, "The mister sounds a right old sourpuss though."

Marya's heart thudded. It was finally going to happen. She was finally going to contact Timothy Hunter, the great magician!

Annie uncovered the phone. "Is this Mr. Hunter?" she said. "It is! Well, I'm calling on behalf of a young woman who's traveled a considerable distance to see your son."

Marya nodded. That was certainly true. She wondered how much farther she was going to have to travel.

"Actually, I don't know why," Annie said. "Why don't you ask her yourself."

She held the phone out to Marya. Marya stared at the odd-looking thing for a moment, then wrapped her fingers around it, blinking with confusion.

It was lighter than it looked. Marya turned it back and forth in her hands, puzzling over how to best use the talking device.

"Hello?" she said tentatively, her mouth midway between the two circular ends.

She heard a voice coming out of one side. She quickly brought that end up to her ear. "Hello?" she repeated.

"What's this all about?" a gruff voice demanded. "Has Tim caused more trouble?"

The man in the telephone sounded harsh and angry. It made her stomach tighten. She reminded herself that she was terribly close to finding Timothy Hunter. That made her feel braver.

"No, it's nothing like that," Marya explained. "I just want to talk to Timothy. It's important."

"Tim's not here. He never seems to be here these days."

"Oh. Maybe he's not there because you're so angry," Marya suggested. "Would it be all right if—"

Marya heard a click, then an odd, flat buzzing sound.

She lowered the phone. "He stopped talking. Now there's just this buzzy noise."

Annie took the phone, listened for a moment, then hung up. "I'm afraid he's rung off on you, dear." She glanced down at the phone book. "Well, if I had to live in Ravenknoll, I'd probably be a grumpasaurus, too."

Marya's green eyes widened. "You mean that book tells where he lives?"

"You bet." Annie nodded. "Thirty-four Traven House, Ravenknoll Estate. That's a Council home. I've got an *A-to-Zed* of London down here. I'll show you where it is."

Annie reached under a counter and pulled out a book of maps. She flipped it open. "See, that's where we are now. And that's where your Timothy Hunter lives."

Marya stared down at the squiggly lines. *So this is London*, she thought. *Somewhere in this jumble of streets lives a master magician. And it's my mission to find him.*

Annie went to wait on more customers, and Marya studied the pattern of the map, memorizing names and turns and directions. Satisfied that she knew her way, she hopped off the stool and slung her pouch over her shoulder.

"Thank you for everything," she told Annie. "For getting my bracelet back, and especially for helping me find Timothy Hunter."

"You're leaving? Planning to walk all that way?" Annie asked, a concerned expression on her face. "You don't even have shoes."

"Oh, I do," Marya explained. "I just don't wear them. Not for walking anyway. Bye now."

Marya strode out the door, ready to resume her mission.

"Wait," she heard Annie call behind her. "I get off at eleven. I could take you . . ."

Marya waved but didn't look back. Now that she knew where Tim was, she wasn't going to let anything deter her. After talking to Timothy's father, she thought Timothy might welcome the chance to escape to Free Country.

Marya walked and walked. She stood on a corner beside a woman pushing twin babies who were howling miserably in their pram. Marya noticed that on the other side of the unhappy babies, there was a scruffy-looking dog, sniffing in the gutter.

Marya grinned. This was an easy problem to solve!

She tapped the lady pushing the pram. "Excuse me?" Marya said. "The babies want to pet the dog over there." She pointed to the dog in the gutter. "But they can't because they're tied up too tight. That's why they're crying."

The woman stared down her nose at Marya. "That filthy mutt?" the woman said.

"Why are they tied up like that?" Marya asked. "Are they crazy? At the palace they tied up Uncle Grigori because they thought he was crazy. He wasn't, though. Just different."

The woman recoiled a bit, as if Marya emitted an unpleasant odor, then hurried away.

"See you later, alligator!" Marya called after her and her howling children. A girl in Free Country always said that, and Marya loved the phrase. Marya waited for the woman to shout back the proper response—"In a while, crocodile"—but she didn't. The woman and her babies vanished into the crowd.

Marya knew she still had a long way to go. She walked along crowded streets. Some of the shops in this area had goods sitting out in front, taking up space on the sidewalk. A little boy reached for an orange on a low display table. Before his fingers closed around the fruit, the man with him jerked the boy so hard the child nearly tumbled over. "Stop that!" the man snapped, smacking the boy's hand. Marya was surprised that such a little boy didn't start to cry. Then she realized the boy was used to this treatment.

Marya rounded a corner. She stopped to let three girls about her age charge past her and up the steps of a small, old building. They were chattering in a lively fashion, and each had a bag slung over her shoulder. Of all the people she'd seen since leaving Annie's café, these girls were the first to seem truly alive. They glowed with something that lit them up from the inside.

Curious, Marya peered into the large, dirty window—and gasped.

If Marya ignored the street around her, she could have easily imagined she was watching a scene from her own, previous life, back home in St. Petersburg.

A dozen or so girls in identical tight black uniforms stood in the room, waiting for a dance lesson to begin. Each girl had her hair pulled back from her face. Some of the faces looked nervous, others calm. One girl was eyeing another, trying to pretend she wasn't studying her rival practice pirouettes. Several preened in front of floor-to-ceiling mirrors, while two girls purposefully kept their backs to their reflections.

A door swung open and a tiny, thin woman with silver streaks in her severely-pulled-back bun stepped into the room. Instantly, the girls assembled themselves into rows. A young man carrying sheet music followed her into the room. He sat down at a beat-up old piano in the corner.

The ballet mistress clapped her hands, the man played some chords, and the girls began the familiar opening barre exercises.

Marya shut her eyes and clutched the railing, her head swimming. It was hard to watch, filled with reminders of her old life. But the pull from that room was impossible to resist. Marya opened her eyes again and watched the girls. When they finally took a break, Marya had to force herself to remember her mission.

She dragged herself away and continued walking. The streets got dirtier, the houses shabbier and closer together. There were more vacant lots filled with trash, more empty buildings with boards over broken windows.

The dingy surroundings pushed hard on Marya's skin, squeezing images of the ballet class right out of her. Her pace slowed, as the oppressive air and the dismal sights weighed her down. Her feet hurt and her muscles groaned. Her pouch now felt as if it weighed a thousand pounds, and the strap etched a groove in her shoulder.

She glanced up at the street sign. She was close. The streets were emptier now and the few people on them were more careless with themselves. Ragged clothing barely stayed on their slouching bodies.

Marya stood on a corner and her heart sank. She faced street after street of identical buildings. How would she ever know which was Tim's? She had forgotten the number.

"Eeep!" She let out a small shriek as she felt a hand grasp her bare ankle. She shook off the hand and stared at the young man who had grabbed her. He lay on the ground, his back supported by a trash bin. He didn't look much older than her.

"What's in the bag, moggie?" he asked. At least, that's what she thought he had said. It was hard to tell, his words were so slurred.

There was another boy, also a teenager, slumped against the wall. He was laughing at nothing, just staring in front of him and laughing.

"Nice moggie," the boy in front of her said. "What's in the bag? Pretty bag."

Marya reached into her pouch and tossed an apple at the boy. He picked it up and stared at it as if he'd never seen an apple before. *Maybe he hadn't*, Marya thought. He was terribly thin, and his hair was purple and green. But now that he had released her ankle, he didn't seem that scary. She peered into the alleyway. The boys seemed to live there, so they must know the neighborhood.

"Do you know where Ravenknoll Estate is?" Marya asked.

The boy turned the apple around and around in his hands. "You're lucky, little moggie. Next corner, you're there."

"Thank you." She took out another apple and handed it to him. "This is for your friend."

She turned away from the strange, lost boys and went looking for Ravenknoll Estate.

"Oh, Tim, poor Tim," she murmured. "I do believe Kerwyn is right. You will be better off in Free Country."

Now that she was here, Timothy Hunter's house number popped back into her head. She stood and stared at the sad house in front of her. She couldn't even guess what color it had once been under the grime. A sagging wire fence stretched between two equally dismal lots. A smashed-up car squatted in the run-down driveway.

He lives here, she told herself. It was hard to imagine anything as wonderful as magic surviving in such a place. *The palace was exquisitely beautiful*, she reminded herself, *and it was full of cruelty nonetheless. So perhaps, even in such squalor, magic can thrive.*

Marya stepped carefully along the broken

pavement; her bare feet were now grimy. She knocked on the door. Marya could hear loud voices inside and music. Perhaps they didn't hear her knock. She tried again.

Finally she decided no one was going to answer the door, so she sat down to wait.

She rummaged through her pouch and pulled out the ballerina statue Daniel had given her. "Are you okay?" she asked the small dancer.

"You can't help it if you can't really dance," she whispered to the statue. She thought back to her dancing lessons in St. Petersburg. It hadn't been the shoes that had held her down, Marya knew that now.

"Poor little doll." Marya murmured. She hugged the statue close. Dolls can't dance. They can only pretend. That was the reason for Marya's failure right there. All Marya had been for the Empress was a doll, a plaything. Marya had never believed in herself.

She remembered the day she had left the palace for Free Country. Kerwyn had arrived as a missionary. He had been doing just what she was doing now. He had left Free Country to spread the word and bring children in. Kerwyn had found Marya crying after the dancing master had called her an oaf and beaten her. Kerwyn found her and told her that he could take her to a place where dreams could come true. Even dreams like hers.

So she went. Only it hadn't turned out quite as she had expected. She never managed to forget the way her mother used to sing to her on summer evenings while she brushed Marya's long red hair. Or the way that you could draw faces in the frost on the palace windows in wintertime. There was too much she missed. That's what held her down now. Even in Free Country. She could never dance like the Shimmers. She was too tied up inside.

And Marya wasn't in London because Timothy Hunter had somehow cried out to Free Country. He was part of a plan. She looked around at the place where Timothy Hunter lived. *Or maybe he is crying out*, she thought. Marya knew if she lived in this place, she might be crying all the time.

She sighed. And wondered how much longer she would have to wait.

Chapter Six

TIM HAD LEFT THE PLAYGROUND and the strange girl with the missing brother ages ago. Titania's stinging words kept spinning around in his head. His shoulders sagged with each footstep, thinking what a mess he'd made of things. What's the good of having magical abilities if you mess things up? And now he had the Faerie Queen on his case. As if Bobby Saunders at school wasn't bad enough.

As he turned onto his block, Tim spotted a slight, pretty, red-haired girl sitting on his doorstep. The sun was going down, and she shivered a little. Her arms and legs were bare and her pink dress looked thin. She stared down at a little statue. Her wide green eyes looked sad. Maybe she had a missing brother, too.

"Excuse me," Tim said. "Are you all right?"

"Are you Timothy Hunter?" the girl asked.

"Uh, yes." *How does she know my name?* he wondered. She looked nicer than the girl in the playground. There was something gentle in her eyes.

"Then I am all right," she said. "I've been trying to find you all day. But I don't think your father wanted me to. When I talked to him on one of those phone contraptions he sounded angry and then he buzzed at me."

"He buzzed?" Tim sat down beside her. He was having trouble making sense of what she was saying.

She nodded. "Uh-huh. Then I walked here and found your house, but I knocked and knocked and no one answered. Even though there were voices inside."

Okay, that part he could figure out. "He probably never heard you over the television," Tim explained. "Sorry about the phone part. He can be a real jerk sometimes." Tim glanced over his shoulder at his front door. *I guess the sensitive pseudo-dad act is over*, Tim thought.

"Well, maybe he can't help it," the girl suggested. "He's a grown-up. They have problems."

"True." The pretty girl had no idea how true that was. Especially all the grown-ups around Tim. "What's your name?"

"Marya." She took two apples from her bag

and held one out to Tim. "Here."

Tim eyed the apple warily. In Faerie it was dangerous to eat anything or to accept gifts from the Fair Folk. This could be doubly dangerous: It was a gift of food offered by a stranger. But this girl was human, not fairy, no matter how odd she seemed. And this was the real world—or at least *his* world, and not Faerie. Besides, if she had been magical, she would have bristled at being asked her name.

Tim had learned that names carried power. He was supposed to ask What are you called?—it was considered more polite. But the girl never noticed his error in magical etiquette. That gave him confidence.

He watched as she took a crunchy bite of her apple. They were probably okay then. Tim hesitated one more moment, then bit into his. It was the most delicious apple he'd ever eaten. Nothing seemed to happen to him, so he took another bite.

"You haven't told me why you've been looking for me," he said.

The girl seemed very surprised. "You don't know?"

Tim shook his head. "How could I?"

"I thought when you were magic you knew all kinds of stuff."

"Don't I wish." Ever since Tim had discovered

that he was magic, he'd continually felt like a sham. Everyone acted like he had all this power, and maybe he did—or would—but he sure didn't know how to use it. Or how to do anything much. He shook his head. "That's not how it is. All it really is is confusing. And complicated. And people all seem to want something—like to kill me."

Then it sunk in—she knew he was magic. He went back on alert. Could she have been sent by Titania? "You don't want to kill me, do you?" He peered at the apple through his glasses.

The girl giggled. "Of course not."

"Then why are you here? And how do you know I'm, well, magic?"

"There's a place," she said, "a place where we can go when we need someplace to go. That's why I'm here."

"We?"

"People who aren't grown-ups yet. Kids. Us. Kerwyn says it's a sanctuary, but it's really just a place. We call it Free Country."

Something about this sounded familiar to Tim. Not in a I-read-this-in-a-fairy-story way. No, something more recent. More real. Tim chewed slowly, thinking it over. Of course! Free Country. The girl in the playground, Avril, had mentioned a free country. That's where the strange child had wanted to take her friends.

Marya had a faraway look in her eyes as she continued speaking. "Nobody hurts you there," she said wistfully, "or makes you do things you don't want to. Nobody ties you up or beats you. Or tries to kill you, like they do here."

"What does this have to do with me?" Tim asked. He stood and paced in front of her. Was she offering him a different world to live in? Had she guessed that it was grown-ups who seemed to be ruining his life? Could Free Country be a sanctuary for him, too? Away from Titania's threats and his own confusion?

"They need you," Marya said. "I mean, *we* need you. We need your magic to help us let all the children in this world cross over to Free Country."

So this wasn't about what she was offering him—it was about what he could give them.

Tim whirled around, his hands on his hips. "Why?" he demanded.

"Because this world is getting so bad that pretty soon it might not be a world anymore."

"Oh, you're sure about that," he scoffed. Those were some seriously dire predictions. *And Molly accuses me of being all doom and gloom*, Tim thought. *She should hear this girl.*

Marya shrugged. "You live here," she said. "What do you think?"

Tim looked around and tried to see his environment, really see it. He blotted so much out as a daily habit.

When he allowed himself to see it, the misery and the poverty, the anger and the sadness could be found everywhere. In his dad's smashed-up car that still haunted the driveway, the ruined lives in the surrounding flats, in the very air he breathed.

Tim sank down beside Marya on the step. "Yeah," he admitted. "I guess I see some problems in this world." He looked directly at her. "But what if I don't want to go?"

"Then you don't go," Marya replied. "You don't *have* to do anything. That's the point. That's why it's 'free'—you're free to choose."

Tim studied her face. She seemed to be completely sincere. It was up to him. He could go or not. Having the decision left to him—and him alone—made him much more willing to go.

Maybe I should, he thought. *Maybe I actually can help. There should be a place for kids to go if they're not safe here. And even if I don't save their whole world, at least I can track down those missing kids, like Avril's brother, Oliver.*

Tim thought back to something he had learned from his real father, Tamlin: that he shouldn't let fear get in the way of trying. That was the way with magic—and the only hope of getting better at it.

"Okay," Tim said finally. "Uh—I'm not sure I can actually help, so don't get all bent out of shape if I fail. But I'm game if you are."

The girl smiled a beautiful, sunny smile. She pulled chalk out of her bag and drew a hopscotch grid on the pavement. Tim stared at her. *Now what is she doing? She is certainly full of surprises.*

"You go first," she instructed. "It's easy. You just hop the hopscotch squares three times and then you're there. Nothing to it."

Tim pushed his glasses back up on the bridge of his nose. He raised an eyebrow at the girl. How could playing hopscotch land him in another world? He'd seen the little kids doing it in the schoolyard regularly and none of them had vanished. She must be using special chalk or something.

"It doesn't hurt," Marya assured him. "And it's not hard."

Tim shrugged. There was no use trying to figure it out now. He stepped up to the hopscotch grid. "Um. I just jump?"

"Well, there's a rhyming, too." She cocked her head and looked at him a moment. "People who say 'uhm' a lot have trouble with rhymings sometimes. I'll chant for you. Ready?"

Tim glanced around to be sure no one was

watching. Only girls played hopscotch in this neighborhood. Satisfied that they weren't being observed, Tim nodded. "Ready," he declared.

Tim heard Marya chanting an old nursery rhyme:

> *"Half a pound of tuppenny rice,*
> *Half a pound of treacle.*
> *Mix it up and make it nice,*
> *Pop goes the weasel."*

Tim concentrated on hopping the pattern correctly. Two feet, one foot. Two feet, one foot. Marya continued chanting more nursery rhymes, some Tim knew, like "One, Two, Buckle My Shoe," and others he'd never heard before, all about kings and queens and emperors.

For one moment Tim wondered how he would get back home. *Marya had traveled back and forth*, he assured himself. *It must not be too hard getting between our worlds*.

Two feet, one foot. Two feet, one foot, two feet, one foot. Gone!

Marya watched Tim jump the pattern and vanish.

He's awfully nice, she thought. *He might truly be able to help Free Country*.

She knelt down and began to erase the chalk marks with the hem of her dress. *Maybe he'll even be able to turn Daniel happy inside.* She sank back onto her heels. *Or maybe not. Maybe magic can't do things like that. Any magic. Maybe nothing can just make you what you want to be. You always have to help the magic along.*

The hopscotch pattern was smeared enough to be unrecognizable. She had accomplished her mission. "Good-bye, Free Country," she said.

She stood and clapped her hands together to get off the chalk. She knew exactly where she was headed: to that dance school. *Some of the girls in that window were spinning around, only wishing they could dance. But some of them were dancing. Really dancing.* Finally, she might be able to find someone to show her how.

Maybe it has something to do with being allowed to grow up, Marya thought.

After living for over two hundred and fifty years, she believed she might be ready for that.

Chapter Seven

DANIEL LEAPED FROM his raft to the riverbank. He had sat in Marya's tent for so long that
he was late for the meeting of the high council.

It seemed Marya had been gone awhile.
*Makes a cove lonesome and skittery inside not to
have her about.* The tent was sure empty without
her. In fact, to Daniel, all of Free Country was
empty without Marya in it.

He ran through the tall grasses, knowing full
well how peeved Kerwyn would be by his lateness.

"Hey!" Daniel yelped and tumbled face forward onto the ground. He lay stunned for a
moment. "Cor," he exclaimed. "What happened
there?"

He sat up and discovered he'd been tripped by
a thick, gnarled tree branch. "That's funny," he
said, rubbing his scraped palms together to lessen
the sting. *Free Country usually never lets that sort of*

thing happen to a fella. Usually, Free Country moves roots and fallen limbs or branches right out of a bloke's way. He patted the soft dirt. "Losing your touch?" he joked.

He scrambled back to his feet and made his way more carefully to the clubhouse where the meeting was taking place.

As Daniel approached he could hear voices jabbering. It sounded like everyone was speaking at once. Daniel grinned. Perhaps Kerwyn wouldn't even notice his tardiness—he'd be much more furious at the talking out of turn. Kerwyn loved his own rules and orders.

Daniel grabbed the soft, thick rope that hung from the upper branches in the enormous tree that held the clubhouse. He gripped it hard, then hoisted himself up to the first wooden slat that led to the entrance.

Kerwyn and Aiken Drum had built the clubhouse in the sprawling branches, aided by Free Country. As new children arrived, the clubhouse transformed to reflect their wishes. There were nooks and crannies for those who liked hiding, turrets for those who enjoyed castles, big tall windows to let in light for those who wanted it and small low windows for the littler ones.

It's a right regular castle in the sky, Daniel thought, reaching the entrance to the main room.

No matter how often he saw it, he was always impressed. He swung his legs through the opening and dropped into the clubhouse. Everyone was already here.

Jack Rabbit, in his extremely realistic bunny outfit, leaned against a wall. Daniel always found it a bit disconcerting to be chatting with a rabbit taller than himself. Sometimes he wasn't even sure that the bunny thing was a costume—it was that convincing.

The kid all in green sat at one end of the table, scowling. One-handed Wat was on Kerwyn's left, and the stuck-up Griselda was on Kerwyn's right.

Freaks, Daniel thought. *The lot of 'em.* Then he had a worrisome idea—did that make him a freak, too? Was the high council for the biggest misfits of all? Is that why Kerwyn had asked them to be part of the group? And was that the reason Marya would never kiss him? At first, Daniel had been honored to be one of the kids in charge—the ones who had important meetings and made decisions and all that. But now, glancing around the table, it made him fidget.

Kerwyn sat in his usual spot at the head of the table, holding a carved wooden staff—the "talking stick," he called it. Daniel didn't know where it had come from. He was fairly certain

Kerwyn hadn't carved it. Pretty smiling faces peered out from the top of the stick. They reminded Daniel of the Shimmers or maybe angels. Kerwyn clung to it as if it were made of gold. It was almost his favorite thing, besides the clipboard that sat on the table in front of him, and the Scrabble game.

"The high council of Free Country will now come to order," Kerwyn declared. "When I call your name, please say 'present.' Daniel?"

Phew. Just in time. "Present, Kerwyn."

"Jackalarum, also known as Jack Rabbit."

"Present."

"Junkin Buckley?"

"Kerwyn, you can see he's not here," the kid in green grumbled.

"Quiet, Peter," Kerwyn scolded. "You have not been announced as present yet. Anyway, I've got the talking stick and I don't recall pointing it at you." He cleared his throat. "Junkin Buckley did not respond," he announced formally. He made a mark on the paper on the clipboard.

"Hullo, my darlings, here I am." Junkin Buckley appeared in the entrance of the club-house.

Daniel started. He hadn't heard Junkin Buckley come in. Junkin Buckley was always sneaking up on a situation.

Junkin jumped down to the floor and gave a bow. "Loverly Junkin Buckley has popped up, pretty as a picture. You can write that down, too." He winked at Kerwyn.

Kerwyn scowled. "You're supposed to say 'present.'"

"I said, I'm here." Junkin Buckley sat down in the empty chair beside Daniel.

"Not 'here,'" Kerwyn insisted, "'present.'"

"Will you please get on with it, Kerwyn!" Daniel sputtered.

Sometimes Daniel enjoyed watching Junkin mix it up with Kerwyn. Kerwyn could be right stuffy and priggish. But today Daniel was irritated by Junkin's casual air. Marya was still in the Bad World. There was important business to be taken care of at this council meeting.

"You're not to speak, Daniel. You know that," Kerwyn scolded. "Only if I point the stick at you may you speak."

"Thou art dawdling, Kerwyn," Wat said. "Shove off with thy foolish stick."

"Exactly," Daniel muttered.

Kerwyn took a deep breath. He pointed his stick at the figure in green. "Peter, also known as Puck?"

"Not present."

"Don't be foolish. How can you be not present?"

"I'm tired of this Peter Pan or Puck, or whoever it is I'm supposed to be. You know I only agreed to wear these stupid tights so that we could get the little fairy over here."

Daniel was glad that none of his missions had required him to wear any dopey disguise. For instance, he would have hated having to wear that bunny suit to bring in animal lover Maxine. But Jack Rabbit didn't seem to mind. He had the outfit on when Daniel had first seen him, and had never taken it off that Daniel knew of.

If it was me, Daniel thought, *I'd be out of that blooming bunny gear right quick*. Though, he did admit, lots of the kids coming over found dress-up outfits and stayed in them. Some days Free Country looked to Daniel like one big fancy dress ball.

"Since we've had to send the fairy back," Peter Pan continued, "I think I ought to be allowed out of this ridiculous getup. And I want to go back to my real name, Katherine." She stood up and glared at Kerwyn. "Got it?"

Kerwyn winced. "You're *really* meant to make your report after roll call, not before. Once the meeting's over you can make a proper request to change back into being a girl."

Junkin Buckley laughed. "As for me, I'm hoping she goes back to being a girl right immediate, and begins by taking off her boy clothes right now." He sidled up to Katherine.

Katherine brought her fist up to Junkin's chin. "Just what do you mean by that, creep?"

Junkin held up his hands. "Hey, I be on your side."

"Toad licker," Kate snarled.

"Kate, Kate, I can't wait. You're the catch and I'm the bait." Junkin Buckley circled Katherine, chanting, "I see London, I see France, I see someone's underpants."

Daniel prepared himself for a serious row. In fact, everyone must have had the same idea. They all leaped up from the table, worried that this might come to actual blows. Everyone started talking at once.

This is unusual, too, Daniel realized. He'd never seen an actual fistfight in Free Country. Squabbles, sure. But no violence. It was as if the very air wouldn't allow it, normally. Something had changed. Free Country wasn't doing her bit to keep those two from fighting.

What did prevent Kate and Junkin from fighting was the total chaos of the meeting. As everyone started shouting, Junkin stopped taunting Katherine. *He probably figured she couldn't hear him over the din*, Daniel thought.

Junkin circled the table, then sat at the end opposite Kerwyn.

"All right. Where's my stick gone?" Kerwyn shouted. "Who took it?"

"Don't you dare accuse me!" Griselda shrieked.

"Why would anyone bother to take that stupid stick?" Katherine said.

"Peace, all of you," said Wat. "End this strife."

"I tell you, someone's stolen my talking stick!"

"Kerwyn, this is becoming tiresome," Wat warned.

"But somebody's—"

Wat lost his patience—something else Daniel had never seen before. "Free Country dies whilst you argue your petty rules of order. Now hold your tongue and let Peter, who is also Katherine, speak."

Kate crossed her arms over her green tunic. "Well, basically the fairy couldn't adapt. Sort of like if we tried to live on the moon. She was getting sicker the longer she stayed here. But we managed to grab some of her power before we sent her home. So, I'm done. I want to change back to being me." She flung her green feathered hat across the room. Her dark hair tumbled down around her face.

"I—I—I demand you keep on your disguise," Kerwyn fumed.

"You'd look better in a disguise," Katherine muttered.

"You are out of order," Kerwyn snapped. "You're done talking."

He slammed the clipboard down hard on the table.

Daniel wanted to smack all of them. Why didn't they get on with what mattered? Marya was out there—somewhere. What were they going to do about that? And if she couldn't bring in Timothy Hunter, she was banished. Forever. Daniel didn't know what he'd do if she never came back.

"Everyone listen," Kerwyn began.

"Shut up, Kerwyn," Jack Rabbit said. "If you're so keen on talking, why don't you tell us how well your team's doing?"

"Aye, how does your band fare?" Wat asked. "How goes the hunt for our great master magician?"

Kerwyn stared down at the table. "I, uhm, I didn't exactly send a band."

"Your company, then?" Wat persisted. "Your team?"

"Not really a team either, exactly."

Wat looked confused. "But did you not send your best fellows to find Timothy Hunter?"

Kerwyn's shoulders slumped. "I sent Marya."

"Marya?" Jack Rabbit repeated. "One girl to convince the mightiest of magicians?"

"She . . . uh . . . she had this plan and . . ."

"Is Timothy Hunter here in Free Country?" Jack Rabbit demanded.

"Not exactly," Kerwyn admitted. "Not yet. But he will be."

"What were you thinking?" Wat asked. "You know how important this mission is. Perhaps the most important of all!"

Daniel had had enough. Kerwyn wasn't about to own up to anything. "What his nibs isn't saying is that Marya forced his hand by swiping his precious Scrabble tiles. She said if he didn't send her to find Tim he'd never see them again. And now I'm worried about her. She should have been back by now." Daniel approached, until he stood over Kerwyn's chair. "If anything's happened to her, I hold you responsible."

Kerwyn gulped. "It will all turn out just fine," he assured Daniel. But Daniel wasn't reassured.

"You should have sent me," Jack Rabbit said. "Seems I'm the only one capable of getting the job done. Maxine is here in Free Country, as ordered. Happy as a doe in a lettuce patch besides."

"What's this 'only one' malarkey, Mister Bunny Cottontail?" Junkin Buckley tipped back his chair and placed his feet on the table.

Daniel glanced down to see Kerwyn's reaction. Kerwyn's eyes narrowed, but he didn't say anything.

"I've gotten Suzy over here, right enough," Junkin Buckley continued, "all on my own. Not needin' a disguise, I might add. All I does is says 'Suzy-poozy, I'm Junkin Buckley, I am.' And I plucked her right from under the oaky nose of— Well, more would be telling, and Junkin Buckley knows when to keep his gob shut." He clasped his arms behind his head.

"Can you tell us more precisely where this Suzy waits?" Wat asked.

"Well, now, that's for me to know and you to wonder about, ain't it? At least for now." Junkin lowered his chair with a thud. "You see, I've got a few questions of my own to be answered. And you have to answer, because I have the talking stick!"

Junkin held up Kerwyn's carved staff.

Kerwyn leaped from his seat. "My stick! You slime-skinned sneaky—"

Junkin Buckley twirled the staff in his hands. It looked strange—wrong somehow, though Daniel couldn't quite make out how.

"Now I wants to know what's this secret plan, then? You said you'd tell once I got the Suzy girl here. You promised. What about it, then? What's the secret?" He pointed the stick at Kerwyn.

"Rules is rules, gov. You have to speak when I point at you."

Wat and Kerwyn gasped. Now Daniel could see what was funny about the stick. The angel faces were now contorted and twisted, seeming to scream in pain and agony.

Everyone in the room moved away from Junkin.

Junkin Buckley's pale eyebrows furrowed together. "Why are you all looking at me that way? What did I do? I haven't done a thing 'cept what you begged me." He dropped the talking stick to the ground and clasped his hands together as if he were begging. "Pleeeeease, Junkin Buckley," he whined, "be my best friend. Pretty please."

The stick rolled over to Daniel. He bent down to pick it up, then hesitated. He didn't want to touch those nasty faces. His eyes widened. The faces had gone back to normal, as if once Junkin Buckley let go it had gone right again. As if something in Junkin Buckley's touch was . . . twisted.

Daniel picked up the stick and silently handed it to Kerwyn. His and Kerwyn's eyes met over the stick as they realized the implications. The stick was passed among the others.

Junkin stared at them, as the silence filled the clubhouse.

"Why won't you speak?" Junkin Buckley demanded.

"None of us will speak while you remain, Junkin Buckley," Wat said.

"What have I done?" Junkin Buckley asked. "I ain't done nothing, I tell you."

"It is not what you have done, Buckley," Wat explained. "It's what you are. You are not one of us. We cannot trust you."

"Not one of you?" Junkin Buckley looked dismayed. "Of course I am. I'm good old Junkin Buckley."

"You need to leave," Kerwyn said. "You are banned from the council, Junkin."

Daniel watched Junkin's face go from surprise to hurt to anger. He lurched to his feet and tore out of the clubhouse. "You'll be sorry!" he called over his shoulder.

The council stood silent for a moment.

"I don't like this," Katherine said. "He might do something to ruin everything."

"Have faith," Wat said. "While it is alive, Free Country will watch over us. As we care for her, she will care for us."

Wat sat back down. "Soon all that we have dreamed these many years shall come to pass. Soon all the world's children shall be here, and free."

Chapter Eight

TIM GAZED AROUND at the extraordinary place he found himself. One minute, he'd been jumping hopscotch in grimy, gray London. The next he stood in a field of bright green grass under a brilliant blue sky with what looked like lollipops growing out of the ground.

"Huh," Tim grunted. "So that's what all those nonsense rhymes are about. They're magical incantations. Interesting."

For one moment he wondered if he was in Faerie. It had changed each time he had popped in for a visit. But, no, there was a different energy here. Tim wasn't sure of its source, but he could sense it. *This must be one of those multiple worlds Titania showed me before she decided she wanted to kill me*, he mused. *I wonder how many more there are?*

Tim took a deep breath. The place smelled of baked sweets and safety. Tim felt his shoulders relax for the first time since he'd been approached by the Trenchcoat Brigade and told of his magical destiny.

"You're right, Marya," Tim said. "This place is amazing."

When she didn't answer, he turned around. And around. And around again. No Marya.

"Marya?" he called. Tim figured it would take her a few minutes to get there. *We probably can't both go through the gate—or door or whatever it was I slipped through—at the same time.*

Tim didn't mind waiting. He lay down in the grass and soaked up the extraordinary sense of well-being it gave him. He felt as if he could simply lie there and all would be set right. All his problems—his two so-called fathers, Titania's rage, how to handle his magic—none of it seemed important right now. What seemed important was that the sun was shining overhead and the birds were chirping a pretty melody that he could almost sing along to.

This relaxed state of affairs only lasted for a few minutes.

Tim sat up abruptly. "Where is Marya?" he muttered. It occurred to him that the whole thing might have been a trick. The idea dismayed him. Marya hadn't seemed to be the sneaky sort. But you never know . . .

Then another grim idea leaped into his crowded brain: Something could have happened to her back in London. It wasn't as if Ravenknoll Estate was the safest place for a barefoot girl who was a stranger to the city. Should he go back and see if she was all right?

But how could he do that? He'd never traveled by hopscotch before. And it wasn't as if he could draw a grid in the grass, even if he had any chalk.

The first time Tim had traveled to Faerie, he'd had a guide and was led through a gate. After that, he'd used the Opening Stone his father, Tamlin, had given him. That seemed to help him travel from world to world. But he didn't have the amulet on him. So how would he get home from Free Country?

Tim stood and stretched. *Better start searching for a way out, Tim,* he told himself. *You may have made one great big blunder.*

He climbed up a small hill to get a better view. He could see kids off to the east, splashing in a lagoon around what looked like a pirate's ship. To the west he saw thick forest.

He spotted a group of kids a few hills over. He'd go and ask them how to get home.

He made his way toward the little hill through trees full of sweet-smelling fruit. All around him

were beautiful and peaceful sights. The place was
quiet and clean. Nothing like back home. Here he
could hear himself think. Not that that was nec-
essarily good. He could hear himself think much
too loudly. And what he was thinking about was
quickly reversing all the calming effects Free
Country had wrought on him.

He walked between the peach and apple
trees. *Funny*, Tim observed, *some of the fruit looks
like it is rotting*. He came out of the orchard and
could now better see the group of kids. They were
on top of a little hill.

*They look like they're dressed for a play or a cos-
tume party*, Tim observed. He glanced down at his
dusty jeans and black T-shirt. *I wonder if I'm under-
dressed*.

A tall dark-haired boy seemed to be the
oldest—about fourteen—and he clutched a clipboard. He wore the kind of poofy shirt and black
leggings Tim had seen actors wear in
Shakespearean plays at school. A girl dressed like
Peter Pan in green tights, green tunic, and feathered cap stood next to a girl in a long, old-fashioned blue dress with ruffles. A blond boy about
Tim's age stood nearby, wearing a tattered overcoat and striped, patched trousers. *Well, at least
someone else isn't all fancied up*, Tim thought. Perhaps the strangest kid of all was the one wearing

a long linen tunic. He was quite short and one of his arms ended in a nasty-looking stump.

"Anyway," the boy in the poofy white shirt was saying, "when he, er, *manifests*, I shall go up to him and say 'Welcome to Free Country, Timothy Hunter.'"

Huh? They're talking about me? Tim's pace quickened.

The Peter Pan girl covered her face and shook her head. "Kerwyn, really. You have got to be joking."

"What's wrong with that?" Kerwyn demanded.

"First of all, you don't call a proper wizard by name," the girl replied. "Second of all, why should you be the one to greet him?"

The girl in the old-fashioned dress nodded. "One finds oneself concurring with Katherine-Peter on this."

Tim wondered if her tightly wound blond curls gave her a headache. That could explain her snooty expression and voice.

"Not Katherine-Peter," the Peter Pan girl snapped. "Just Katherine. Sheesh!"

The snooty girl rolled her eyes. "Katherine, then. It should be Wat who has the honor of initial address. He is the most well-mannered." She bowed to the short, one-handed boy.

So his name is Wat, Tim thought. *What kind of name is Wat? He must have been teased a lot in school.*

Wat shook his head. "I must respectfully decline this honor, good lady. Public speaking suits me not."

Since they're having so much trouble deciding who gets the great honor of greeting me, Tim thought, *I'll just introduce myself. Save them time arguing, which means I might get home sooner.*

"Uh, hello," Tim called. He jogged the rest of the way up the hill toward them.

None of them responded.

"You see, Griselda," Kerwyn said, "it should be me. And as I was saying, I shall go up to Timothy Hunter and say—"

"Sorry to interrupt you," Tim tried again. "But—"

Kerwyn glared at Tim. "Will, er, someone please explain to this individual with the spectacles that he cannot hang about here? Daniel?"

The boy with long blond hair and the tattered overcoat held up a fist. "Bugger off," the boy snarled at Tim. "We're waiting for someone important."

Tim took a few steps backward. This seemed to satisfy the group, and they turned their backs on him, making their circle a little smaller and tighter.

What is up with these kids? Tim wondered.

"Now where was I?" Kerwyn said.

"You was about to greet Tim Hunter, Kerwyn," Daniel said. "And then the minute you do so, I ask about Marya's whereabouts."

"She may be with him," Wat said. He lay his hand on Daniel's arm. "Don't worry so."

"Actually—" Tim began.

Daniel whirled around, fight in his eyes. "Didn't I tell you to back off, mate?"

Tim held up his hands in a placating gesture. He took a few more steps backward, but he continued to listen. He needed to figure out what was going on.

"Yes. Right. So I shall say, 'Welcome to Free Country . . .'"

"'Mighty wizard,'" suggested Katherine.

"'Noble sir,'" said Daniel.

"'Magisterial mage,'" the little guy, Wat, added.

"So which is it?" Kerwyn asked. He sounded exasperated.

"How about 'Hi, thanks for coming,'" Tim muttered. "'And sorry we're a bunch of rude sots.'"

"A tricky question," replied Griselda. "The fellow is a master of the magical arts. One must ascertain whether or not he derives income from this practice."

"I doubt that he does," said Wat.

"Why would that matter?" Kerwyn asked.

"Etiquette would demand a different greeting were he in trade."

"Excuse me!" Tim said. *Sheesh. Am I invisible or something?*

"Since he is not a merchant," the stuck-up girl with the tight curls continued, "one would suggest you begin, 'Welcome, Lord Thaumaturge.'"

"Lord what?" the girl in green asked.

My question exactly, Tim thought.

"And then, of course," Griselda continued, "you would present him with the keys to Free Country."

"Keys?" Kerwyn clutched his clipboard to his skinny chest. "We don't have any keys."

Tim had had enough, despite Daniel's threatening attitude.

"I said, excuse me!" Tim poked Griselda on her shoulder. She shrugged him off, then waved her hand in the air as if she were shooing away a fly. She didn't even bother to look at him.

"A medal, then, or a ribbon," she said, "some

symbolic token of our affection and respect."

"Well, I'm not giving him one of my games," Kerwyn said. "Maybe we can find him something in the library."

"Good idea. How about a first edition?" Griselda suggested. "My tutor was always quite pleased whenever he received such a gift."

Hm. A book sounds good, Tim mused, *depending on what kind of story it is.* "Why don't you just ask me what kind of present I'd like?" he asked. He didn't get an answer. By this time he had quit expecting one.

Kerwyn looked worried. "We don't have any first editions, do we?"

"Well, you can't just give him some old book," Katherine argued.

"I know!" offered Daniel. "Why don't we give him Kerwyn's talking stick. E'll 'ave a lot of talking to do come the invocation."

Tim's eyebrows rose. *Invocation? What invocation?* But he knew better than to ask.

"Daniel, you really don't have a clue, do you?" Katherine scoffed.

They're all clueless, Tim decided.

Daniel looked ready to smack Katherine. "What did you say?" he demanded.

Wat pushed his way between them. "Come, come, my friends," he said in a soothing tone.

"'Tis not meet that the one we intend to honor should find us squabbling."

"Wat is right," said Kerwyn. "What matters most is our plan."

"Yes." Wat nodded. "Soon enough all the children of the Bad World will be in Free Country."

Bad world? Did Wat mean London?

At the mention of the Bad World, each of the kids shivered.

"They kill children there," Daniel said.

"They think that because we're smaller and weaker than they are that they can do whatever they want to us," Katherine said.

"In the Bad World," Griselda added, "all children live by adult rules. They choose if we live or if we die . . . if we are to be beaten, starved, or put to work at the age of eight."

"Or younger," Daniel said in a low voice.

"With Timothy Hunter, we will have the power to end the tyranny," Wat declared. "This is our mission. This is our crusade."

"Our crusade!" the others chimed in.

"If we have Timothy we have magic," Kerwyn said. "And if we have magic, we have the master gateway to allow in all the others."

All of the children nodded solemnly.

"We will meet later, to finish choosing our words and ceremonies," said Wat.

And with that, the group dispersed without a glance at Tim.

Tim stared after them. He felt completely invisible or at any rate deeply insignificant. "Bet this sort of thing never happens to John Constantine of the Trenchcoat Brigade," he muttered. *And Molly would never stand for their rudeness either.*

So now what? he wondered. *How am I supposed to get home? And where is Marya?* Obviously she'd been telling at least a partial truth: This group of kids wanted him for something. But the fact that she hadn't returned with him could mean that she had plotted this whole thing as a way of escaping from Free Country. Which would imply there was something to escape from.

After listening to that group of kids, it was clear to Tim that Free Country was where Avril's brother, Oliver, had gone, along with all the other missing children. *But did they come by choice? Or were they coerced or tricked or kidnapped?* Tim had certainly come of his own free will, but if Marya wasn't around to show him how to get home, how much free will did he really have?

His would-be greeters had scattered in different directions. After being treated worse than a bug by that crew, Tim decided he didn't want to follow any of them. He was on his own.

"If I were a gate to another world," he said, "where would I be hiding?"

As he walked he tried to piece together what he knew so far. It wasn't much. The kids of Free Country wanted him because they thought his magic would help them with their plan to bring kids from home into Free Country.

"They're going to be disappointed," Tim said. He had no idea how his power could help them do anything.

He hated this feeling—like he was letting people down, dashing expectations.

"It's not fair!" he cried, stamping his foot. The loudness of his voice startled him, and he quickly glanced around to see if anyone heard him. There was no one in sight.

"I never promised them anything," he muttered. "They're just assuming. So if it goes badly, they've no one to blame but themselves."

He kept walking, unsure of what to look for. "Don't see any hopscotch grids. Or chalk, for that matter," he said. He hadn't a clue what a gate from Free Country would look like. "So, Tim, what did you do in Free Country?" he asked himself out loud. "Funny you should ask, Tim. I spent a lot of time talking to myself."

He stopped walking. "What's this?"

An enormous hedge blocked his path. "This

looks like it could be guarding something," he said. "Maybe a gateway to home." The hedge was about ten feet high and neatly trimmed.

Tim walked all around the hedge. The shrubbery was so tightly grown together he'd need gardening shears to get inside. It was perfectly square, like a bright-green leafy box. At one side he found a trellis archway, completely overgrown with vines sprouting enormous flowers. It looked as if it had once been an entrance.

He reached out his hand to touch a bright purple rose.

"Don't touch!" the flower snapped at him.

Tim jerked back his hand, startled. He shook his head. *Why does anything surprise me anymore?* "Sorry. I was just interested. I wasn't going to pick you or anything."

"Well, then, it's okay, I guess."

Tim peered at the rose. This time it didn't seem as if the rose had been the one speaking. There must be someone on the other side of the hedge.

"You can come in if you want," the voice said.

Tim's eyes widened as the plants, flowers, and vines uncurled. He stepped inside the hedge box.

He spotted a small green girl, high in a tree. At least, she was sort of a girl. She seemed more like a plant. Her body was smooth, like a plant stalk, but she had legs and arms like a regular person. But the hair sprouting from her head was thick grass. Tim noticed tiny flower buds dotting her hair. She was small, about the size of an eight year old.

"Did you make the plants do that?" Tim asked. "Just move out of the way like that?"

"Uh-huh."

"That's a neat trick," Tim commented. "What else can you do?"

He hoped she'd say "get you home without playing hopscotch," but instead her chin quivered as if she were about to cry.

"I think something's wrong with me," she choked out.

"Why? What's the matter?"

"I don't feel real here. Everything smells different and there's nothing good to eat. And Junkin Buckley lied. I hate him and I want to go home." She ended in a long wail, covering her face with moss-colored hands.

Tim sat under her at the base of the tree. "Madam, I know exactly how you feel."

"You do?" She spread her fingers apart and peered down at him.

"More or less. At least, I want to go home, too."

"Really? You're not one of them?"

"Nope," Tim said. "I am most definitely not one of them. And wouldn't want to be."

Her face brightened, and one of the buds in her hair opened. "Then we can play dolls together. This bush grew them for me when I started to cry."

She pointed below her to the bush beside Tim. He'd been so struck by the girl's appearance that he hadn't noticed that little baby dolls were poking out of the bush.

"Dolls. Right. Makes as much sense as anything else." *A girl who's a plant. Grass that grows lollipops. Now this. Be prepared for anything*, Tim warned himself.

The girl floated down from her perch in the tree. She hovered above the bush.

Make that a plant girl who can also fly, Tim amended his previous statement. *She is definitely from one of those other worlds—way other.*

The girl plucked the dolls from the bush as if they were flowers. "I'll have this one and this one and this one." She studied one, then held it out to Tim. "You can have her."

"Thank you, I guess," Tim said. "So what's this dolly's name, then?"

The girl smiled. "That's Oak Leaf. For bravery. That seems to fit you." She clutched two dolls to her chest and hugged them. "I've got Veronica

and Honeysuckle. For fidelity and affection." She
pointed to a doll that was peeking out from under
a rock. She flew over to Tim and whispered into
his ear. "That's Peony. For shame. She lives under
the rock."

This is one elaborate game, Tim observed. *And
I thought my identity problems were complex.* "Did
you make all that up by yourself?"

The girl laughed. "Course not. It's the language of flowers. Everyone knows that."

"No, they don't. I don't."

The girl looked extremely surprised, then
shrugged. "Everyone used to know, then. They
sent each other messages," she explained. "Like
bluebells means 'I'll always love you,' and jas-
mine means 'we're friends.' And asphodels . . ."
She shivered. "Asphodels are for the dead."

Tim stood up and stretched. "Listen, I wish I
could stay and play with you but I really do have
to find my way back home."

"Don't you like it here?" she asked.

"No."

"Me neither!" the girl exclaimed. "So why did
you come?"

"A girl named Marya talked me into it. It
seemed as sensible as anything else at the time."
Though it seems really, really dumb now, Tim admitted to himself.

"Where is she now?" the girl asked.

Tim sighed. "I have no idea."

"What's it like where you're from?"

"You ask a lot of questions, kid."

"You're being rude. Don't call me that."

"Sorry. What should I call you?"

"My name is Suzy. And you should be nice to me because the same thing happened to me that happened to you."

"What do you mean?"

"A boy named Junkin Buckley brought me here, and then he disappeared," Suzy explained. "I want to go home, but I don't know how. Just like you. So I found a place to be and things grew all around me. And I just broke my doll." She dangled the doll above Tim.

"What?" Tim asked.

"When I broke a doll before, I just held it out in front of me and it got fixed. Now it's not working." She showed it to Tim. "Can you fix her?"

Tim glanced at the doll. Suzy had subconsciously snapped off the doll's head while she was talking. *She must be seriously peeved at this Junkin Buckley chap.* "Why don't you pick another?" he suggested.

Suzy's chin quivered again. "Because I like this one," she said plaintively, holding it out to Tim.

Reluctantly, Tim took it. Examining it from a

number of angles, he could see that the only way to repair it was with magic. But could he even do that?

He held the doll and concentrated. He thought back to when he had first used magic, to keep the snow from falling on Kenny, the homeless man. *Don't think about anything but the space between the neck and the head*, he told himself. *Close it up with your mind. The edges reach for each other; they want to be joined, they belong as one.* Over and over Tim found words to command the doll's neck and head to fuse—to use its former wholeness to repair itself.

"She's all better!" Suzy cried, breaking Tim's focus. He blinked a few times at the doll.

"Hey, you're right. Here." He handed the doll—now in one piece—back to Suzy.

"Thank you, thank you, thank you!" Suzy fluttered all around him.

Tim grinned. It felt good to make the little flower girl so happy, when only moments before she'd been in tears. And it felt good to use his magic successfully—without dire consequences, without anything going wrong as a result. Maybe he'd be able to figure out this whole magic thing someday after all.

"Well, now that you have your doll back, it's time for me to go." He took a few steps away from Suzy.

"Can I come with you?" Suzy asked.

Tim turned around. He gave the girl an amused smirk. "I really don't think we're heading in the same direction. I mean, I'm from London and it's pretty safe to assume you're not. And I'm not really in the mood to visit any strange botanical kingdom. So good luck, and I hope everything works out for you."

He turned around and started walking. Maybe if he found a place that was more citylike or at least had pavement, he could try that hopscotch thing again.

He thought about Suzy. *What an odd little creature*. He felt bad about leaving her behind, but what could he do? Trying to help Marya got him into this mess. Who knows what would happen if he tried to help a plant girl? Besides, he didn't want to be distracted from his mission to get home.

But something was distracting him now. A shadow of a small girl with wild grassy hair was visible on the ground in front of him.

"You're following me, aren't you," Tim stated.

"No," Suzy replied.

"Well, go away. You're not coming with me, all right?"

"Fine."

Tim walked a few more yards. He turned

around, put his hands on his hips, and glared at Suzy.

"I'm not following you!" she insisted.

"Now look—" Tim began, exasperation rising.

"But you're my boyfriend!" Suzy exclaimed. "We go everywhere together. You can't stand to be without me, not even for a second."

Tim was so startled by this that he stared at her, openmouthed. There was really no way to respond. He turned around and went back to walking.

"Suzy! Please don't follow me," he called over his shoulder.

"Okay."

Now he didn't even bother looking at her. He kept his eyes straight ahead. "You have to turn back," he insisted.

"All right."

"And I'm not your boyfriend," he added for good measure.

"I know."

This was becoming absurd. Becoming? No, it was *already* flat-out ridiculous. *How can I fight a girl who agrees with everything I say, then does what she wants anyway?*

"You're still there, aren't you?" he said.

"Maybe."

Tim sighed. *I give up. I'm stuck with her. I just hope it doesn't become a horrible disaster to have her tagging along.*

"So what kind of flowers are asphodels, anyway?" he asked.

"Daffodils."

Hm. I wonder why daffodils are for the dead. "So how does the language of the flowers—"

A scream from Suzy cut him off. He whirled around.

"What's wrong?"

"Stop him!" she cried. "Oh, please. We have to stop him!"

She darted past Tim, heading down a hill to the lagoon. Now it was Tim who was following her. He had to run fast to keep up.

"What's wrong?" he called. "Who do we have to stop?" He really hoped it wasn't some dark practitioner, wizard, or ogre. He'd be really bummed if those types were also allowed into Free Country. What would be the point of a refuge if it didn't keep you safe?

"A flower is hurting!" Suzy shouted back.

"A what is what?" Tim slowed his pace. *This rescue mission is to save a flower?*

Suzy flew back to Tim and tugged on his arm. "Come on! He is pulling the petals off. They're screaming at him to stop. He can't hear."

"Whoa," Tim murmured, staring at the lagoon.

Mermaids frolicked with dolphins, while kids played on an old pirate ship. Everyone was splashing and happy.

Everyone except for the chubby little boy sitting on shore. He sat, frowning, doing exactly what Suzy described. The kid had a pile of daisies, and he was plucking the petals from each of them.

Probably pulls the wings off flies, too, Tim thought.

"Okay, I'll stop him," Tim assured Suzy.

"Of course you will! Because you're my boyfriend hero!"

"Whatever."

"Hurry," she urged. "Do you hear the flowers? They're saying, 'Oliver, stop! Please! Stop!'"

Oliver? So maybe this unpleasant-looking kid was Avril's missing brother. He even sort of resembled her.

I might as well do my good deed for the day, Tim thought as he approached Oliver. *This kills two birds with one stone. I can make Suzy happy by getting Oliver to quit destroying her flower friends, and then if I manage to find a way home, I'll get Oliver back to his family.*

Well, that's a pretty big if, Hunter, Tim told himself.

Tim strode over to Oliver. "Hey, Oliver. Please put down the flowers."

"Won't." Oliver gripped the stems in his thick fingers and scowled.

"I'm not asking you, Oliver. I'm telling you." There was something about this kid that brought out the irritated parent in Tim. He reached down and pried Oliver's fat fingers apart.

"Ow!" Tim yelped. He stared down at Oliver who was now grinning. "You brat! You bit me!"

The boy stuck out his tongue. "You taste bad!"

Tim rubbed his hand. At least the kid hadn't drawn blood. Tim handed the flowers to Suzy. "Here you go."

"Thank you!" She hugged the flowers close and cooed over them like long-lost friends.

Tim faced Oliver again. "Okay, kid, like it or not, you're coming with me."

"Won't. You're horrid."

"That's right. I am. But you're still coming with me."

"You're a big pile of doggie doo."

"Actually, Oliver, I'm Tim Hunter. And I know your sister, Avril. She's very worried about you."

"Avril is doggie doo, too."

Tim rolled his eyes. *Why am I even bothering?*

"Timothy Hunter's my boyfriend," Suzy informed Oliver. "He's a master magician. He fixed my doll. So you better do what he says or he'll turn you into a toad."

"Ooooooh!" Oliver's piggy little eyes widened. "I know something you don't know," he chanted in a singsong voice. "I know something you don't know."

"And what's that?" Tim demanded.

"I know something you don't know! I know something you don't know!"

"Okay, Oliver, you're getting on my nerves." Tim snarled. He reached for Oliver's ears. "Shall I try to see if your ears are detachable?"

"I'll tell!" Oliver yelped. "Don't hurt me."

Tim smirked. His bluff worked. Finally *something* was working.

"A boy said if we met a boy named Tim Hunter or a girl named Suzy who was like an orchard, we should tell somebody right away."

Oliver's beady eyes narrowed into slits with a nasty gleam in them. "They're gonna catch you. You're in big trouble now."

Chapter Nine

"THEY'LL BE SORRY," Junkin Buckley muttered as he crashed through the dense shrubbery of the forest. "Where do they get off? Sending me away like I was rubbish. Yesterday's fish and chips."

He shrugged. "No matter. Things will be different soon enough!"

Thinking about the future lifted his mood. Instead of crashing on twigs and branches with stomping feet, he practically danced through the woods.

"Hubsy-bubsy wokka wobsu hipsy-dipsy bokka rubsy," he chanted, picking up his feet in little jiglike steps. He stopped and looked around, searching the dark woods for the landmarks he'd memorized.

Almost at the meeting spot, he realized, hurrying along.

I know there's need of secrecy, but did the old guv'nor have to choose such a shadowy wicked dark place for us to meet?

He stopped again. *This is the place, ain't it?* He peered around. *Yup! There's the gnarled oak tree— there's the stump scarred by lightning.* "Anybody there?" Junkin called. "Hello? Yer honor?"

"Good evening, Junkin Buckley." A man wearing heavy cloth robes emerged from the shadows. Not a boy—a man. An adult. In Free Country.

Junkin Buckley had been afraid Free Country wouldn't allow him to bring in the geezer, but she did. After the old gent had made him the offer, Junkin knew he'd do whatever it took to help the man. Free Country's vigilance must have grown a bit spotty, and in hopped the old gent, with no one the wiser. No one but wise Junkin Buckley, that is.

Junkin hopped onto the tree stump. "I was wondering when you'd show yer face. Well, my old darling, everything going according to plan?"

"Of course, Junkin Buckley. All goes quite well. They won't be able to get all the children of Earth across, but I would expect they'll get over a few million before this junkyard collapses and dies on them."

"It's sort of funny, ain't it," Junkin mused. "There they was, getting all uppity 'cause they didn't want me to know their secret plan. And all the time it was *I* who had the secret plan." He jerked a thumb at himself. Then he caught the smirk on his companion's gaunt face. "Well, you and I," Junkin added. He ducked his chin and swung his legs in embarrassment. "Well, you."

A slow smile spread across the man's face, revealing his yellowish teeth.

"Do you know what they will pay in the distant markets for living human children?" the old gent asked.

This is what Junkin Buckley liked to hear. He liked hearing about money.

"Lots and lots? Lots and lots and lots?"

The man licked his lips as if he'd tasted one of Free Country's delicious fruits. "Even more than that. This will be the most remarkable and the most profitable operation ever."

He clamped his hand on Junkin's shoulder. "Think on it," the man crooned. He waved his other hand in front of Junkin Buckley's face as if he were painting the scene in front of him. "Those little fools open the great gates, convinced they're doing the right thing, convinced that the children of Earth need rescuing. With Timothy Hunter's help, millions of human children will tumble across to Free Country. But Free Country cannot sustain them all. It can barely sustain the lives and fantasies of the brats here now. It crumbles and dies as more of them come."

He laughed a harsh laugh. Junkin tried not to care that the sound sent a few shivers up his spine. Not one bit. He was thinking about the money.

They'll be sorry, Junkin thought. *I could have stopped all this. But I won't. Not now.*

The man rubbed his gnarled hands together. "Then my people will come in and round up all the children from this dead world. It will no longer be able to protect them. Then I will sell them in the distant markets at great profit!"

Junkin wondered if this old gent could really carry out this whole plan. Though what did it matter, really? If only a little part of the plan worked, he'd have shown up those spoilers. And he'd be rich.

"You have played your part well, Junkin Buckley. You will be rewarded for this."

Junkin Buckley hopped off the tree stump. "You know what I wants. I gets first choice of all the girlies. As many girlies as I wants." Junkin paced in front of the man, imagining what else he could have. "I know! I gets a big palace house by the seaside a long way from Free Country." He stuck his thumbs into his suspenders and puffed out his chest. "And I gets a big medal saying that Junkin Buckley's the best bucca in all the world."

The man smiled. "It will be arranged. Now I have to be sure that those brats don't manage to lose Hunter, now that they've finally got him here. For any of this to work, it is his power that we'll need most of all."

The moment Tim got Oliver to admit that they were in the exact spot where he had first arrived in Free Country, Tim drew a hopscotch grid in the sand and tried to open a gate.

One big problem, Tim thought. *I never did like nursery rhymes, so it's bloody hard to remember any.*

He started hopping. "Uh, 'Old Mother Hubbard, sat in a cupboard, eating her curds and whey'?"

Oliver snorted. "That's not how it goes. Loser."

"Then you do the rhyme," Tim snapped.

"Won't!"

"Oliver, I am warning you," Tim said, hoping to sound threatening.

"Old Mother Hubbard lives in a shoe," Oliver chanted. "Old Mother Hubbard is a great big poo!"

Tim shook his head. *How do I get into these messes?*

Suzy fluttered above him. Tim didn't think she had once set foot on the ground since they'd arrived at the lagoon. He wasn't sure if it was because she didn't like sand or if she wanted to stay out of Oliver's grubby reach. "So what do we do now, boyfriend?" she asked.

"Suzy, please."

"Sorry Tim. Timbo. Timmy-wimmy."

"Just Tim's fine." He sighed. "I try again, I guess." He erased the hopscotch grid and drew another. He wanted to start fresh. He shut his eyes and tried as hard as he could to recall a nursery rhyme—any nursery rhyme.

"Pease porridge hot,

Pease porridge cold,

Pease porridge in the pot,

Nine days old.

My mother says to pick this one, so out goes Y-O-U!"

I got all the way through a rhyme! Don't quit now, he told himself. Marya had had him hop the grid three times.

He repeated the rhyme, and on the third time, he jumped and slammed into something invisible. He landed hard on his backside and stared at the place that he had banged into. But there was nothing there.

"Hah-hah!" Oliver laughed. "You fell on your bottom."

Tim stood and brushed himself off. He crossed to the invisible barrier and reached out his hand. Only there was nothing there at all now. Just air.

Hunh. That is wicked weird.

It had felt as if he had banged into a closed door. So maybe the rhyme worked, only the gate was shut. And since he stopped hopping and chanting, the doorway vanished.

"Maybe there's another gate somewhere?" he wondered out loud.

"You're a master magician," Suzy said. "Can't you do a spell?"

Tim groaned. *Why are people always counting on me to do things—things that I don't even know how to do?* It was too much pressure. He had totally, thoroughly, and completely had it!

"For the last time," Tim shouted. "I'm not a blasted master magician and I don't know any bloody spells."

Tim kicked the sand, obliterating the hop-scotch grid. *Who needs it anyway? Bloody useless.*

"The biggest magic I ever did was to keep snow from falling on an old man," Tim fumed. "Oh yeah—and I turned my yo-yo into an owl."

"You turned a yo-yo into an owl?" Suzy asked.

"Yes," Tim mumbled.

"Why? Was there an owl shortage or something?"

Tim sighed. He still missed his owl, Yo-yo.

"It's a long story."

"Fibber." Oliver sneered.

"Shut up, Oliver."

"Liar, liar pants on fire," Oliver taunted, "climbing up a telephone wire."

Tim covered his face with hands. "Oh, please, won't someone just make this kid stop? Oliver, I'm going to thump you if you don't shut up."

Suzy flew straight up several feet. "What's that?" she exclaimed.

"What?" Tim asked. "What's wrong?"

"I can smell something. And the plants think there's something very funny going on."

"The plants?" Tim repeated. He wasn't sure if he was comfortable getting his news flashes from flowers.

His nose wrinkled. He smelled something odd, too.

"I smell a farm!" Oliver shouted. "Or poo. It's poo!"

Tim glared down at him. "Shut up, Oliver."

Something very serious was going on, indeed. The ground shook, and Tim could hear rumbles and animal howls. And they were getting closer.

Suzy flitted around frantically, and Oliver crept up behind Tim and gripped his blue jeans with sticky fingers.

Tim's eyes widened and he gulped. An entire

menagerie was approaching. Leading the group was an elephant—with a small, dark-haired girl riding its back.

Okay, the elephant girl was pretty impressive. But the animals with her just plain freaked Tim out. Tigers, lions, giraffes, wolves, monkeys, bears—all of them moving steadily toward Tim, Suzy, and Oliver.

"Make them go away!" Oliver wailed.

Suzy doesn't seem afraid, Tim noted, *just curious*.

The girl on the elephant held up a hand, and the procession of animals halted. Tim could feel sweat running down his back. It took a lot of effort to keep himself standing still, but he figured it was a whole lot safer than trying to make a break for it.

"Are you Tim Hunter?" the girl demanded.

"Yes." It didn't seem worth it to lie or refuse to answer. Not with all those salivating mouths and large, pointy teeth just a few feet away from him.

"I am Maxine," the girl said. "The high council wants to speak with you." She turned toward Suzy. "Are you Suzy the flower girl?"

"Maybe," Suzy replied.

"They want to talk to you, too."

Oliver slid out from behind Tim. "I told you,"

he gloated. "I told you they were going to catch you."

Maxine stared down from her high perch. "Who are you, squirt?"

Oliver's expression went from smug to terrified. He plopped down on the ground. "I'm Oliver Crispin Hornby Mitchell and I want my mummy." He stuck his thumb in his mouth.

"Well, I suppose you'd better come along, too. Bothersome as you are, we can't leave you here."

"We can't?" Tim muttered under his breath. Oliver glared at Tim.

Maxine lifted her hand, and the animals started moving again. "Turn around and walk straight ahead," she ordered.

Easy for her to be bossy, Tim thought. *She has the entire animal kingdom as enforcers. And in this weird world, the animals even understand English.*

"Suzy," Tim whispered. He glanced behind him. The girl on the elephant was too far back to hear him, but he didn't want to take any chances. "Suzy, you can make a break for it. Just fly away."

"And leave you on your own? Never!"

"That's very sweet of you, Suzy, but, really, you should get away."

"I don't want to. I was all alone before you came. I like it better to be with you. Besides, if I ran away they'd just chase me. And I still haven't figured out how to get home."

"I guess you're right." Tim's brow furrowed as he tried to come up with a plan. "How about this: What if we all make a break for it? You distract them, I'll grab Oliver, and we'll run into those woods over there. You hide for a while, and once you think the coast is clear, come find us."

"I have the smartest boyfriend in the whole wide world." She flew down and kissed him on the cheek.

Tim knelt down beside Oliver. "Okay, kiddo, hop up. Time for a piggyback ride."

Oliver's chubby face brightened. "Goody. My feet hurt."

Oliver clambered up onto Tim's back and flung his arms around Tim's neck.

"Yow! Not so tight."

Oliver's grip loosened a little.

"First rule," Tim told Oliver. "Don't strangle your ride."

Oliver kicked Tim. "Go fast!" he ordered.

"Don't worry," Tim murmured. "We will."

Tim looked up at Suzy and nodded. She winked back at him.

"Can't catch me!" she trilled. She soared straight up above the treetops, then veered away from the thick woods.

"Stop her!" Maxine cried.

Perfect. Suzy had created a decent diversion. The whole herd was changing direction. "Hang on," Tim hissed to Oliver. He raced as fast as he could into the woods.

Uh-oh. Tim heard howls and roars, and he knew the animals were after them. At least using Suzy as a decoy had bought them a little time. He put on speed. His chest felt tight and his muscles burned.

He heard strange cries overhead. He glanced up, and his heart sank. Eagles and hawks had flown after Suzy. He hadn't noticed any birds in that menagerie. They must have been farther back.

Now his heart thudded for a different reason. *Man, I just blew it big-time. I've probably managed to get us all killed. Killed and eaten.*

Still, he kept going. He leaped over a downed tree limb, then dropped to his knees. Clutching one of Oliver's hands to be sure he didn't lose the kid, he crawled into a thick bramble bush.

He hunkered down in the thorns. Oliver clung to him, shrieking at the top of his lungs.

"Shut up!" Tim ordered.

"Don't yell at me!" Oliver wailed. "I don't like this. Not one bit."

Tim took a deep breath. It wouldn't help to shout at Oliver when he was trying to get the annoying kid to shut up. "Listen, Oliver," he whispered. "We don't want them to know where we are. We're playing a serious game of hide-and-seek. Okay? And if you're the quietest one of all you win."

"A prize?" Oliver asked.

"Yes," Tim replied, "a great prize. Fantastic. The very best."

"Chocolate?"

"Sure."

That seemed to work. Oliver was quieting down.

Tim could hear the animals getting closer. Tim held his breath as several creatures ran past them. He hoped none of them could hear his heart pounding. Or smell the sweat beading up on his forehead, his upper lip, his back.

Suddenly, hot, meaty, breath on the back of his neck alerted him that they'd been discovered. Tim slowly turned his head.

And stared into the yellow eyes of a tiger, who looked awfully hungry.

Chapter Ten

TIM PANTED HARD, trying to breathe through Oliver's suffocating clutches.

Well, one side benefit of fear, Tim thought. *It finally shut Oliver up.*

A roar, and the tiger was joined by a leopard. And then a lion.

They each sniffed, coming so close that Tim could feel their whiskers, could smell their pungent animal scent.

Okay, if there ever was a time for magic, Tim told himself, *that time is now. But what do I do? Make ourselves disappear? Make* them *disappear?* Fear made Tim's brain go a mile a minute; first one idea would occur to him, then another and another—all in the space of seconds.

"Uh, tiger, lion go away," Tim began, trying to figure out some kind of chant or spell. "That is what I have to say."

He shook his head. *How lame can you get?* he admonished himself. He could feel his own heart and Oliver's thudding hard.

The lion and tiger seemed to be having a roaring competition. The leopard sat on its haunches and watched them for a moment. Then its intense focus shifted to Tim. It began to creep closer.

"Stop!" The girl who had been riding the elephant stood behind the animals. "Stop, I said. We must bring these three to the high council. We must not delay any longer."

The tiger, the lion, and the leopard each gave Tim and Oliver a long hungry look, then turned. The tiger's tail flicked Tim's nose.

"Hey!" Tim yelped. He rubbed his nose. That tiger's tail had a powerful swing.

"Is the game over now?" Oliver asked.

"Yes," Tim said, dragging Oliver to his feet. "The game is over now."

He spotted a familiar shadow on the ground. When he turned around, he saw Suzy floating above them. A long vine was tied around her wrists. Tim realized Maxine held the other end of the vine. She'd captured her.

"Come," Maxine said. "They're expecting us."

Tim filed past her, defeated, Oliver clutching his hand.

"I'm sorry, Suzy," Tim said.

"That's okay, Timmy-wimmy. You tried your best. That's all a girlfriend can expect of her boyfriend."

He didn't bother to correct her again about that boyfriend stuff. Not after he had blundered so badly and put her at such risk.

At length, they arrived at a clearing where an elaborate clubhouse sat in the enormous branches of a massive tree. The kids Tim had seen squabbling about his arrival stood there, waiting expectantly.

They must have heard us coming, Tim thought. His nose wrinkled at the powerful animal scent surrounding him. *Or maybe they smelled us.*

Maxine rode her elephant right up to Wat.

"Well done, Maxine," one-handed Wat said. "Truly nobly done."

"They weren't that hard to find," Maxine replied. "My friends got them pretty easy. So here they are. All yours."

Tim could feel hot animal breath on the back of his neck again. He edged slowly and carefully away from the leopard behind him. *If this was a cartoon*, Tim thought, *I'd look like a great big burger reflected in that cat's eyes.*

"Tim, Suzy. I'm Wat."

"We already sort of met," Tim said. "Where was it? Oh yes . . . you were trying to think of a nice way to welcome me. You hadn't quite decided to have me hunted by wild animals back then."

"We do what we must," Wat replied.

"Timmy, are you going to turn them into toads now?" Suzy asked.

"Not yet, Suzy."

"Pity."

Tim thought it was a pity, too. But he guessed that the only chance they'd have of getting home would involve learning more from the inhabitants of Free Country. And they wouldn't be able to help him at all if they were toads. Assuming he could even figure out how to transform them.

"Maxine." Wat addressed the girl on her elephant. "Will you come with us to the high council meeting?"

"I don't think so. I'm kind of tired. I'm going back with my friends for a while."

Maxine handed Wat the vine that served as Suzy's leash. The boy in the overcoat—Daniel, Tim remembered—wrapped a jump rope around Tim's wrists. Daniel must have noticed Tim's surprised expression. The boy shrugged.

"We only have toys in Free Country. No proper weapons." He gave the jump rope a sharp tug, causing Tim to wince. "But we can improvise, can't we?"

Daniel leaned in close. "What've you done

with Marya?" he whispered.

"Nothing!" Tim exclaimed. "She got me to come here and I never saw her again. She's got a lot of explaining to do, if you ask me."

"I didn't," Daniel snapped.

"But you just did," Tim argued. "You said"— Tim mimicked Daniel's cockney accent— "'What've you done with Marya?'"

Daniel shoved a bright blue handkerchief into Tim's mouth.

Okay, Tim thought. *I guess this conversation is over.*

Maxine rode her elephant into the grove she had claimed as home. Here she lived with the bears, monkeys, giraffes, tigers, horses, birds, and cats she had as her chosen companions. If it flew, crawled, galloped, or climbed, it was welcome. As long as it wasn't human.

Maxine slid down from the elephant and addressed her menagerie of friends.

"I thought I ought to wait until we got away from the others to scold you," she declared. "I wasn't about to do it in front of those kids. But Mr. Leopard, I know you were going to eat that Tim boy when he ran away."

The leopard lowered its eyes, its spotted tail flicking.

"You would have," Maxine insisted, "if I hadn't made you stop. But you know how terrible it is to be hunted."

"Like to run and chase," said the leopard. "Like to sniff and follow."

"What we do," said the tiger.

"Rabbit thing tell us if we catch, we eat it," added the lion.

Maxine stared at the animals. "He was lying to you," she fumed. "I don't think I trust Jack Rabbit anymore. He's not a real rabbit, you know."

"We know," said the leopard. "Wrong smell."

"Well, don't trust people," Maxine warned. "And Jack Rabbit is people. Don't trust any human but me!"

"We eat Jack Rabbit?" the tiger asked hopefully.

"No," Maxine said firmly. "I don't like him—or trust him—but it's not good to eat other animals. And a person is just a clothed animal, only less interesting."

The tiger's tail flicked back and forth. "All eat each other. Sometime alive. Sometime dead."

"Eat deer when we catch," explained the lion. "We die, buzzards eat us."

"Would you eat me?" Maxine asked.

"No," said the leopard.

"Yes," said the tiger.

"Maybe," said the lion.

Maxine knew she could not ask them to go against their true natures. Their essence was meat eating. She had been wrong in thinking she might change them. It was unfair that she kept them with her—so close to temptation. It was asking for trouble. She knew it, even if the animals did not.

"I think all you lions, tigers, leopards, and wolves and cheetahs better go away," she said.

"We like to be near you," the tiger protested.

"We want to stay," said the lion.

Maxine shook her head. "Well, I'm sorry, but you can't." She stared down at the ground. She knew if she looked into their beautiful, deep eyes, she'd give in. And she couldn't. She had the other animals to think of. In nature they wouldn't all be living together, prey among their predators. It was only her power that allowed it. But she had to let the carnivores leave.

"I like you all, too," she admitted, "but how can I live with someone who might want to eat me?" She looked up again. "You can still visit sometimes, if you want to."

"Yes," said the tiger.

"We come," agreed the lion.

"Sometime," added the leopard.

"Good-bye," Maxine said, having trouble

getting out the simple word. She cleared her
throat. "And stay away from the other people,"
she warned. "They'll mix up your minds and try to
make you work for them. Or maybe kill you and
use your skins for rugs."

The elephant wrapped its leathery trunk
around her, lifted her up, and set her on its shoulders.

"We'll go away, too," she told the remaining
animals. "Somewhere no one will find us."

They moved forward as a herd—the gazelles
and giraffes, the small cats and birds. The elephant's ambling gait soothed her. "Maybe we can
find a nice place," she said dreamily, "with sweet
grass and nuts and berries. Good stuff to eat.
Better than eating animals or people. With a pool
and a waterfall and trees to climb."

As Maxine described her ideal home, Free
Country provided it. The berries burst from bushes,
the air sweetened with the fresh grasses, and
nuts—already shelled—fell from the trees into the
waiting mouths of squirrels and chipmunks.

"And no other people anymore," she declared,
"all arguing and scheming and telling stupid lies.
These Free Country people are just as bad as
grown-ups. Come on, let's find a good place to
sleep."

The elephant came to a stop in front of a cave.

Maxine slid down the elephant's trunk and peered inside. "It's cozy in here," she declared. She went in, followed by many of her animal friends. A large black grizzly bear lay down and curled up on the floor of the cave.

Maxine crept over to the bear and snuggled into its soft fur. He was her favorite, all warm and cuddly. He reminded her of her daddy.

"You won't eat me, will you?" she asked the bear.

The bear didn't answer in words—he never spoke—but he made gentle, comforting, snuffly sounds.

"I know you eat meat sometimes," Maxine said, "but you don't have to. You're clever—you can choose. I have to choose, too, you know. I have to choose whether to stay here or to go back home.

"I love Free Country. It's the only place where I truly feel like I'm home," she mused. "But sometimes I wish it was even more perfect than it is."

She sighed. "When Jack Rabbit told me how bad I was needed here, I thought all the other kids would come and we'd learn how to save the world. But nobody knows what's happening, and I'm confused again."

One thing she did know, though. She did not trust Jack Rabbit. Not one bit.

Chapter Eleven

TIM SAT IN THE CORNER of the clubhouse. *How did these kids go from treating me like an honored guest to treating me like a prisoner?* The jump rope wrapped around his wrists chaffed and the gag in his mouth was really uncomfortable.

"You should not treat my boyfriend like that," Suzy scolded. She hovered in the air. Daniel had tied her vine leash to the back of a chair. Oliver sat under the table, pouting.

"If we remove your gag," Wat said, "you must promise, on your honor as a wizard, not to utter any kind of magical spell, invocation, or charm. Do you so swear?"

Ridiculous. They want me to swear while a handkerchief is rammed into my mouth. "Mmph. I pho pwhywe ooww aake viff off me."

The kids exchanged puzzled glances. "I

believe that was his attempt to satisfy the terms," Kerwyn said.

"I believe you are right," said Wat. "Daniel, remove the gag."

Daniel untied the knot behind Tim's head, and then Tim spat the handkerchief out of his mouth. *Blech*. His tongue felt all cottony.

He stretched his face muscles and wiggled his jaw a bit. "Are you going to let us go home, then?" Tim demanded, once his mouth was working.

"At this moment, Timothy Hunter," a voice said behind him, "we could not send you home even if we wished to do so."

Tim turned and saw that another kid had just climbed into the tree house. He was dressed like Kerwyn and seemed to be about the same age.

"What news, Aiken Drum?" Wat asked.

"The gates out of Free Country have closed," Aiken Drum said. "We have brought so many through in the last month, she cannot nurture all of them. She lacks the power."

"Who's she?" Tim asked. Was there yet another person for him to worry about?

"Free Country," Wat explained. "She has a spirit, a soul, a heart like any being."

"That explains why the branch tripped me!" Daniel exclaimed.

All turned to face him.

"I was running," Daniel explained, "and for the first time ever, I tripped over a branch and fell. Usually Free Country keeps those things out of the way."

"Is that why she wouldn't fix my doll?" Suzy asked Tim.

"Maybe so," Tim said. *And that must be why I felt as if I'd slammed into an invisible door when I did that last hopscotch,* he realized. *Because I had jumped right into a closed gate.*

"She has grown weak indeed," Kerwyn said sadly.

Wat stepped up to Tim. "Can you not feel her pain, Tim Hunter? Her distress?"

Tim stared down at the short, one-armed boy and shrugged. "Not really. But I'm happy to take your word for it."

The gigantic bunny lurched over to Tim and grabbed him by the front of his T-shirt with enormous pink paws. "Are you trying to make a joke of this council, boy?"

It was very hard to take a threat from an oversized bunny rabbit seriously. "Not particularly," Tim replied. "Are you? I mean, dressed like that . . . ?"

The rabbit raised a paw as if he were about to strike Tim.

"Jack Rabbit," Wat said in a sharp tone, "back."

The rabbit released Tim and hopped to the other side of the room.

"If it helps, I'll believe you," Tim said. "The world is dying and now you can't send us back. So what's your point here?"

"Free Country has been our home and our refuge for many, many years," Aiken Drum explained. "But we knew that we were the privileged ones. We were saved and loved. Why we were selected to be rescued we did not know."

Wat took up the story. "But in the Bad World we came from, children were being hurt, starved, killed. How could we live with ourselves if our salvation could not be universal? Thus it was we resolved to save all the children of the Bad World."

"Every one of them has stories such as ours," Kerwyn said, "of abuse, of neglect."

Tim raised an eyebrow. "All? I don't think so." He put his hands on his hips. "You can't tell me that those forty missing children from Brighton each had a horror story. And from what I know of Oliver"—he jerked a thumb under the table—"it's his parents who need the refuge."

Wat's eyes narrowed. "We have created a world for children. This is where they belong."

"But—" Tim began. Then he noticed both Jack Rabbit and Daniel glaring at him. He decided to let Wat continue with the explanation. "Okay, go on."

Wat nodded. "As we began to bring over the refugees, it became apparent that Free Country could not sustain all of them."

"That's where you lot came in," Daniel said. "Jack Rabbit obtained a list of the most powerful children there were in each of the universes that touch ours. Then we set out to bring each of you here."

"Why?" asked Suzy.

"Free Country needs power," Kerwyn said. "Each of you has power. Power we need to feed and save the land."

"You met Maxine, who lives among the animals," said Wat. "She gave us healing power and she continues to aid us."

"As you will, too," Wat said.

"What if we don't want to give you any of our power?" Tim demanded.

"The mirrors will do as they must, will ye or not." Wat signaled to Daniel and Katherine, the Peter Pan girl. They pulled a large black velvet cloth from a tall, ornately carved full-length mirror. They wheeled the mirror over to where Suzy was tied up.

"Are you going to hurt me?" Suzy shrieked. She turned and pleaded with Tim. "Timmy, please don't let them hurt me."

Tim started to move toward her but was restrained by Kerwyn and Jack Rabbit. He stared at the mirror, trying to figure out what was going on. From what he could tell, absolutely nothing.

"It does not hurt, Suzy," Wat assured the panicked plant girl. "You see, it has already happened."

Suzy floated gently down to the floor. She looked weak and pale. "Tim, they took something from me," she moaned. "There was something inside me that isn't there anymore."

"I'm sorry," Tim whispered. He remembered how he felt when his mum died and thought Suzy must be feeling something similar. Why couldn't he work his magic when he really needed to?

"Now you, Tim," Wat ordered.

Tim shook his head. "You lot. You're all stark staring loony."

"Maybe we are. But we can save the children of your world and we can save ours."

They truly are insane, Tim thought. "But you just said that Free Country isn't strong enough to cope with the kids she's got. How's she going to cope with millions more kids from—"

"Enough!" Jack Rabbit bellowed. "We stand

and jabber while our world dies and children of your world burn and scream and perish."

"Tim, this won't hurt or anything," Kerwyn assured him. "You'll just feel a little drained for a bit. We need your power."

"You're the wizard," Wat said. "Your power will change everything."

Nobody ever listens, do they? "I don't have any power!" he shouted. "I'm not a wizard. I'm just me!"

"Show him to the mirror!" Jack Rabbit cried.

The kids surrounded him, grabbing his arms, pushing his legs. Tim struggled against them, but he was outnumbered. They shoved him directly in front of the mirror. Tim squeezed his eyes shut, uncertain what would happen. They held him in place. A moment passed.

"Shouldn't something be happening?" Tim heard Daniel ask.

Tim's eyes popped open, and he faced his reflection. All he saw was himself—a confused, somewhat bedraggled, regular kid from London. He crossed his arms over his chest. "See?"

"But I don't understand," said Kerwyn.

"Thou art the master magician," Wat said.

"I told you I'm not a master anything!" Tim fumed. "I'm still trying to figure out who I am."

Jack Rabbit shoved the other kids aside to stand beside Tim and stare into the mirror. "But it has to work," he said. "I don't understand!" He gripped Tim's shoulders with his big paws and shook him. "You were the power to open the great gates. To bring all the children here. You were the power!"

Tim's eyes widened. This rabbit wasn't only not a rabbit—he was no ordinary kid either. And as badly as the others wanted this to work, the big bunny was almost obsessed.

Then it hit him—this was all a trick. They were using him, like everyone he had encountered since he discovered magic. He didn't care what their so-called cause was. They had no right. No right!

"Look at that mirror!" Kerwyn cried.

Tim stared at his reflection. His mirror self was glowing, and he felt an extraordinary power surge through him. It was as if an electrical current were running between him and his reflection.

Anger rushed through him, and as it did, the reflection glowed brighter—stronger—until it was blinding.

I am sick of being manipulated! How dare they trick us! I can't believe they hurt Suzy. It's a violation, what they're doing. This lot is as bad as the adults they're trying to escape.

He heard shrieks and howls of pain all around him. He could feel the floor beneath his feet shake, as if they were caught in an earthquake, but he never took his eyes off the mirror, never broke his connection with himself.

He heard gasps behind him, and realized the kids in the clubhouse no longer saw his reflection in the mirror. What they were seeing was the destruction of Free Country. Chasms opened up, and terrified animals fled from crevices. Trees shot into the air, as if being spit out by the ground itself. Grass burst into flame.

"Timothy! Stop!" Katherine cried.

"Do you not feel the screams of Free Country?" Wat shouted above the deafening roars. "For her sake, please stop!"

"Anybody! Please! He's destroying the world!"

"Suzy, stop him!" Kerwyn shouted.

"Kill him!" Jack Rabbit ordered. "Somebody kill him!"

Tim watched the terrible devastation reflected in the mirror, not certain of how he was making it happen. It was as if Free Country were erupting.

He heard Suzy's voice whisper in his ear, "Enough."

If I'm doing this, Tim realized, *I can stop it*. He

reached out and touched his reflection in the mirror.

Silence.

In fact, Tim didn't think he'd ever heard such loud quiet in his life.

Chapter Twelve

IF THAT'S A MIRROR, *what was it reflecting about me?* Tim wondered. He took a step backward, and realized he felt very drained. He sat down hard on the floor. Suzy curled up on his lap.

Whatever it is that I did used some serious wattage, Tim realized. *Magic can be that way.*

So far, not one of the children in the clubhouse had moved or said a word. The only one still standing, in fact, was Jack Rabbit. The rest had collapsed to the floor.

"You—you—" Jack Rabbit sputtered. He advanced on Tim, his eyes flashing with fury.

Tim didn't think he had the energy left to fight. He dislodged Suzy and stumbled to his feet.

"You shall pay for this!" Jack Rabbit shouted. He lifted his hand.

But before he could strike, sparkling creatures

of translucent light shimmered in between Tim and the rabbit.

"The Shimmers!" Daniel gasped. "I've never seen them leave their pond before."

"It is done," the Shimmers said. But their mouths never moved, and the words sounded more like musical notes than any language Tim had heard. Yet he understood what they were saying. He glanced around the clubhouse. Obviously, they all did.

Somehow, Tim knew by looking at the beautiful sprites that they were the manifestations of the heart and soul of Free Country herself. They were beautiful.

"It is over," the Shimmers said. "The territory is damaged, but it will survive."

Tim felt relieved. He didn't want to be responsible for any permanent devastation.

"You would have used Timothy Hunter to power the world?" the Shimmers asked. "You might as well attempt to use the heat of the burning sun to toast your bread or to try to force the ocean into a pail."

"What's going on?" Suzy whispered.

"I think we're going to find a way home," Tim told her.

"Most of the children that have been brought across in recent months are already returning to

the world from which they came. Those who
choose to stay, may. Maxine has found her place
here with her beloved animals. Already Free
Country begins to reshape herself."

Tim could sense the relief in the room.

"It is still a refuge," the Shimmers promised,
"but it cannot be a refuge to all. It will take its
refugees as it did in the past—a handful at a time.
Its gates will once again be few and hard to find."

They were hard enough for me to find, Tim
thought. *At least, when I was trying to get out.*

"But—our plan," Kerwyn said. "We wanted to
keep safe the children."

"You must have realized that not all children
need to be rescued," the Shimmer scolded. "How
could you not? There are unhappy souls here, and
that made Free Country weaker as well."

"That's exactly what I tried to tell them," Tim
told the Shimmers.

"But I don't understand," Wat said. "We were
told that the Bad World is not a safe place for children. Any children."

"Even worse than in our times," Aiken Drum
added. "Jack Rabbit said that—"

The Shimmers interrupted. "You are the vic-
tims of a deception."

"Don't listen to them," Jack Rabbit shouted.
"They don't know anything. They're just little

wispy shapes of light. They're not even real."

"Oh, we're real," the Shimmers assured him. "Only *you* are not."

The Shimmers danced around Jack Rabbit, and as they did he changed form. The large pink rabbit transformed into a haggard, pinched man in monk's robes.

"You!" Aiken Drum shouted. "You lured us to the ship! Because of you my sister perished in the sands and Yolande died!" He lunged for the monk.

"Stay back!" The man dashed across the room and leaped out the doorway.

Tim raced after him to see if the man had fallen to his death. He knew how high up in the tree they were. Aiken Drum pushed beside him.

No one lay on the ground. Tim craned his neck in all directions. *He isn't running away somewhere.*

"Where did he go?" Aiken Drum asked.

"I'll have you aboard in a jif!" a voice called out above them. "Hold on just a bit longer, me old gent."

Tim looked up through the branches of the huge tree. His mouth dropped open.

A sailing ship—complete with mast, sails, and crow's nest—floated in the sky. The monk dangled from a line hanging from one of the portholes. A teenage boy with red hair was leaning over the side, one hand on the wheel.

"I told you you'd make a pig's breakfast of it."
Junkin Buckley chortled.

"Let them try to flee," the Shimmers said
behind Tim and Aiken. "Free Country will make
things right. There will be no blood on your hands.
But have no fear, neither the corruptor nor the
corrupted will escape. All is safe once more."

"But our plans—" Wat protested.

"No." The Shimmers were insistent. "It is
over." With that, they vanished.

Tim returned to the rest of the group. "Who
was that rabbit-man-thing?" he asked.

Kerwyn and Aiken Drum gave each other a
long, sad look. "We have seen him before," Aiken
Drum said. "In our time, he was a monk, preach-
ing to children to join the crusades."

Kerwyn shook his head. "To think he found
his way here. And is still in the business of profit-
ing from selling children."

"We have failed," Wat said sadly.

"No. Free Country still lives," Aiken Drum
said. "And that is all we can ask for."

Tim looked out the clubhouse door again. The
Shimmers were right. The countryside was
already restoring itself. The gaping holes in the
ground were closing up, and trees were righting
themselves. He took a deep breath.

"Tim. I feel funny," Suzy said. "Like something's pulling me away. Tim. Please hold my hand."

"Sure thing." He gripped both of her hands. They gazed at each other as she became less and less substantial. Finally, she vanished completely.

"Bye-bye, kid," he murmured. Suzy had been kind of sweet, like a little sister.

Tim felt funny, too, as if his insides were being gently tugged but his outsides weren't quite cooperating. "I think it's time to go," Tim said.

Aiken Drum stepped up to Tim, his hand outstretched. Tim clasped it. "I guess things are back to normal, eh?" Tim said as they shook hands.

"You did a good thing, here, Tim," Aiken Drum said. "You have saved us. And not just us— you have saved those who will still need Free Country in the future. Go knowing that you have protected a sanctuary for countless children."

Tim felt a warm flush color his face. He wasn't sure if it was from the pleasure of hearing Aiken Drum's words or if it had something to do with how insubstantial he was becoming. Things went blurry as he choked out, "Thank you."

Next thing he knew, he was standing on the sidewalk in front of his house in London.

"So Free Country sent us all home," he said. "At least, I think she did."

He glanced around. *Uh-oh. Oliver never came*

*out from under that big table. What if the Shimmers
hadn't realized the kid was there?*

Tim didn't know where Avril and Oliver lived,
but he figured it was probably near that playground where he had met Avril. That seemed like
a good place to start. As much as he detested the
obnoxious kid, Tim knew he'd constantly be wondering if Oliver had ever made it home.

Sure enough, as Tim approached the playground he spotted Avril on the swing and Oliver
digging in a pile of dirt.

"Oliver, stop torturing that worm, you little
creep."

"Won't."

"If you don't stop, I'll make you eat it, pig. I'm
warning you." She looked over at Tim. "Oh. It's
you again."

Tim plopped onto the swing beside Avril's. "I
see your brother has returned."

Avril scowled. Maybe bad moods ran in her
family, Tim observed. "They're all back," she said
in a very complaining tone. "Everyone in the
neighborhood and the whole wide world."

"You might say thank you. I did help get
Oliver home."

"I'm supposed to thank you for that?"

She had a point. Oliver was a nasty bit of
business.

"Besides, you didn't have anything to do with it," Avril said. "It was all on the telly."

"What was?" He could just imagine the news story: *Giant Rabbit fools kids into having a crusade in a magical land. Tries to escape in a flying ship. Film at eleven.*

"On the telly they explained about mass hallucinations. That was where they went."

"What? Don't be daft. You can't *go* to hallucinations—that's not a place."

"Can, too! So says the lady on the six o'clock news." She gave him a dismissive once-over from head to foot. "And looks like you should know—you sound like you were hallucinating, too!"

Tim shook his head in disbelief. He stood up to go. "Bye, Oliver."

"You're still a pile of doggie doo."

Maybe those Free Country kids had the right idea, Tim thought. *Only there ought to be a place to send kids like Oliver, so the rest of us can have a refuge from them.*

Tim trundled home, suddenly exhausted. It took him longer than usual, because he found himself walking very carefully, avoiding stepping on any little plants or grass. When he realized what he was doing, he laughed.

They're not Suzy, he reminded himself. *Still, why crush a plant if I don't have to?*

That got him to thinking about the little sprouts growing at his mother's grave. "I wonder what they'll be when they grow up?"

No way to know. Don't know what kind of seeds they were. I suppose one could say I don't know who their parents are—we have that in common.

Then he stood still. *I'm thirteen years old*, he marveled. *And I've already saved two entire worlds—Faerie and Free Country. Well, that's a story to tell your friends, or at least the most important one. I didn't get to tell Molly today, but there's always tomorrow. I wonder what she'll think. Who would have thought I could save a whole world, let alone two?*

Maybe I have a knack for this magic thing after all.

The journey continues
in *The Books of Magic 4*:
CONSEQUENCES

Free Country

IT WAS ANOTHER GLORIOUS DAY in Free Country, a spectacular afternoon in an eternity of blissful hours. All was well in the sanctuary world, originally created as a haven for children in danger. The lovely spirits who were the heart and soul of this paradise, the Shimmers, danced above their crystalline pond. Children's laughter could be heard punctuating the soundscape, mingled with lapping water, rushing brooks, birdcalls, and wind chimes. This was a world where the formerly deprived, the previously abused, and the perpetually frightened could be happy and safe. Yes, all was as it should be, as it always was.

Or was it?

Daniel sat glumly in a rickety little rowboat, glaring at his fishing pole. His long dark-blond hair was pulled back in a ponytail that poked out from under the battered top hat sitting low on his forehead. He had rolled up his striped cotton trousers and his overcoat sleeves so they wouldn't get wet, but they did anyway. This did not improve his mood.

"Any luck?" Spud asked.

Spud perched in the bow of the boat, facing Daniel, with his fishing line over the side. Daniel was in the stern, gazing unseeing at the high cliffs rising from the riverbanks. It had been Spud's stupid idea to go fishing. Daniel wasn't going to let him get off lightly for such a bad plan.

"Not a nibble," Daniel complained. "You know, Spud, it would help if we had some bait on them hooks."

"Cripes, Daniel," Spud replied. "Any ol' gump can catch fishies with bait! And here I thought you was a sport."

"I'll tell you what I am," Daniel grumbled. "I'm stunning bored, that's what."

"Awww, ain't you a drip and a half," Spud complained. "You're a regular wet blanket these days. Ever since your sweetiepie scrammed out of here."

"Marya wasn't my—" Daniel whirled around on the bench, nearly capsizing the little boat. He settled himself before he continued. "We was *friends*. That's all."

Spud snorted. "Sure. You were just pals. 'Cause she wouldn't have anything to do with the likes of you."

Daniel turned back around in his seat, so that Spud couldn't see his face. He fixed his eyes on a spot on the horizon and counted to ten. His hands balled into fists, despite his effort to stay calm. "What do you know?" he muttered.

"I know more than you think," Spud taunted. "The way I heard it, Marya ran away because you tried to kiss her."

"What?" Daniel rose from the bench without even thinking. He turned and stepped in front of Spud, scowling down at the boy.

"Quit rocking the boat, will you? Do you want to end up in the water?" Spud scolded.

"You take that back," Daniel ordered. He knew he shouldn't let Spud get to him like this— that it would only egg Spud on. But the things he was saying! Daniel couldn't just let that pass.

As predicted, Spud smirked and kept up with his teasing. "Yep. I heard you snuck up on her at Shimmer Rock and gave her a great big ol' smackaroonie! She burst into tears and ran away, clear out of Free Country."

Daniel reached down and grabbed Spud's upper arm.

"Ow!" Spud yelped. "Let go!"

Daniel yanked Spud up off his seat so that they were nose to nose. "You listen to me," Daniel growled. His voice was low and serious. He didn't think he had ever heard himself sound that way before. "I never did no such thing."

For the first time, he saw real fear in Spud's brown eyes. The boy squirmed, trying to get away, and knocked his tweed cap into the water. "Let go," Spud said—only this time it wasn't a command, it was a plea.

Daniel just clenched tighter, with both hands now. Spud stopped struggling and went limp in Daniel's grip.

"You think Marya's gone because of something I done?" Daniel demanded, giving Spud a little shake. "What do you think she took with her as her most special memento? Huh?" He shook Spud again. "The little ballerina statue I gave her. What do you think of that!"

He released Spud, who teetered and then sat down hard on the bench, water sloshing up into the rowboat. Daniel bent his knees a bit, rocking with the boat, keeping his balance.

Spud rubbed his arm and scowled at Daniel. "Okay, okay, you don't have to get all physical."

Daniel knew Spud would have a big bruise on his arm, but he didn't care. Spud had to learn that he couldn't say such things and get away with it.

"So then why *did* Marya leave?" Spud asked moodily.

Daniel's eyes narrowed. He felt anger rise up

in him again, only this time it wasn't Spud he was mad at. "It was that Timothy Hunter," he said with a clenched jaw. "Timothy Hunter lured her away to the Bad World and I hate him for it."

"So why don't you go and get her back, instead of picking on me," Spud complained, rubbing his arm again.

Daniel stared at Spud. He had never realized what a genius Spud was until that minute. He was dead brilliant!

Sitting down beside Spud on the little bench, Daniel clapped a hand on Spud's shoulder. Spud flinched, as if he was afraid Daniel would hurt him again.

"That's just what I intend to do, old chap," Daniel said to Spud, giving him a friendly squeeze. "I'll find her, all right. I'll find that bloody Tim, too. Timothy Hunter will regret the day he ever came to Free Country."